HIDDEN

INTENT

— • —

JANUARY KELLY

To my husband...
Thank you for all the time you have given me to become the best human
I can.

To Church...
My beta reader number one

ALSO BY

Paranormal Romantic Suspense

The Hidden Series:

The Night They Knew- a short story from The Hidden

Hidden Intent

Smoke and Shadow

Relative Deceit—coming soon!

Standalone:

The Last Lament of the Late Shawn Reilly

Contemporary Fiction

All These Days

Three things cannot be hidden: the sun, the moon, and the truth.

--Buddha

www.januarykelly.com

Follow on Facebook:

https://www.facebook.com/profile.php?id=100067850730415

Instagram:

https://www.instagram.com/januarykelly.author/?next=%2F

1

— · —

Derek rolled onto his side and blinked his eyes slowly. He noticed the room was still dim with the last remnants of daylight; shadows cast long and low. The familiar buzzing vibrated on the table next to him. Rolling over, he lifted the phone from the wireless charger and groaned softly.

"Theo," he answered sleepily.

"Hey man...you up yet?" Theo's voice boomed from the other end.

Derek moved the phone away from his ear, "Uh...yeah... Where the hell are you? It sounds fucking loud."

"Oh, yeah, sorry about that," The noise faded and died away. "Better?"

"Much," Derek sat on the edge of the bed.

"So, how long until you get to the shop?" asked Theo.

He looked at the time on his phone and around his room as if gauging how long it would take him to get dressed, "Thirty minutes, I guess... I need a shower and food."

"Alright... We've got a full night...I'll see you there," Theo said as he hung up.

Derek looked up to the ceiling as if searching for a reprieve from a higher power and said to himself, "Yeah, great."

Within twenty minutes Derek had showered, brushed his teeth, ran his fingers through his dark cut of hair, and dressed. He grabbed his phone and keys and headed out of his apartment. The streets of Portland were busy with life as he slid into the driver's seat of his Jeep. It was only about a fifteen-minute walk between his apartment on Bellevue and the tattoo studio on Park, but Derek had no interest in subjecting himself to more people than he had to tonight. The short drive at the very least offered him a little more space and isolation.

The last couple of months had been an out-of-control emotional roller coaster for him. It all began when he and his girlfriend of one-year split ways suddenly. The relationship had not always been the greatest or most stable, but he never thought that she would show up one day and, out of the blue, tell him she had been sleeping with one of her clients for several weeks. If that didn't blindside him enough, the fact she left the studio with two thousand dollars of his equipment and the nasty postings left on all of her and the studio's social media, certainly would. It all escalated quickly into a lawsuit against her, and from there, life seemed to just become shades of grey. Derek was exhausted and numb from the drama and chaos.

Day in and day out he followed the same routine; just going through the motions of life with no real living—studio, food, home, sleep. He wasn't pining for her; he really didn't miss her at all. He felt betrayed, agitated, and bored with the entire situation. His art didn't even give him satisfaction now. He used to always get excited about every single client that came through his door. And no matter how small, unchallenged, unoriginal, or monotonous the piece was, Derek made his clients feel as though they had a one-of-a-kind, original masterpiece. Now, he faked it. Every butterfly, abstract tribal, and skull made him want to throw up and throw in the towel.

Theo tried at every avenue to snap Derek out of the *funk* as he called it, "Dude, let's do it up tonight."

Which was Theo- speak for club-hopping, drinking, and chasing girls.

He tried to reason with Derek, "Man, she's a bitch. Just forget her. She just wanted to use you for the connections... she got what she wanted.... get her out of your head."

But it wasn't that she was in his head at all. Derek really didn't care about her anymore; as a matter of fact, he was glad she was gone. But for some reason, the fallout of all the drama that followed expanded the dark cloud that had already begun to develop around him.

Derek blinked as he pulled up next to the sidewalk that ran in front of his studio. He didn't remember the drive; then again, he could make that route in his sleep. He opened the front door to find Siobhan, his receptionist, assistant, and best all-around friend, already at her station, a smile bright on her round face. He had always been fond of Siobhan; a feeling that was reciprocated fully. They had a very close bond, a kinship of sorts. Neither of them had much in the way of a family; Derek by universal design and Siobhan by choice. Derek always felt he was her protector of sorts, even though she had been on her own just as long as he and practiced what he knew were at least two different types of martial arts. The girl had been through hellfire and could take care of herself; he respected the shit out of her.

For her part, Siobhan was completely devoted to him. She handled all the day-to-day activities for him to help him run his business. She answered phones, booked appointments, assisted in sterilizing equip-ment, did the inventory, and kept his books. She also made sure he ate and remembered to pay the bills. Because they were so close, she knew that he was at the lowest point she had ever seen him. She, for one, never liked the relationship he had with the ex, but she supported him at every turn, after all, he was an adult and could clearly make his own decisions. But when the "*weasel cunt*", as Siobhan now referred to her, used her key to steal from Derek and the business, Siobhan took it personally and couldn't hold her tongue any longer. But that was weeks ago, and his dark cloud still hung over him.

"Hey, Reek! You need a shave," Siobhan smiled at him.

Derek rubbed his cheeks absently, "Yeah, guess I do."

Siobhan stood from behind the tall island counter and handed him a cup of coffee, "Well, if you don't, that goatee will be a beard soon.... here, coffee."

"Thanks," he took the cup from her, sipping gently.

Siobhan took a deep breath, "Reek, can we tal..."

But before she could finish, Derek interjected, "How many tonight?" She gave him a hard stare; he was doing it again.

"Deflection," she said curtly.

He met her gaze and his eyes softened at her disapproval. She knew him better than anyone ever could, and not only could he not lie to her, but he couldn't stand to disappoint her. He smiled in resignation, "Yeah, what's up?"

She nodded toward one of his empty rooms and led him through the door. She hopped up on the large table in the center of the room as he took position on the rolling stool in the corner.

"So... let's talk," Siobhan began. "I know you're tired of hearing me and Theo talk about this, but Reek... you've got to come out of this. This isn't you. You roll out of bed right before you come here.... you're sleeping like fourteen hours a day... you're a goddamn mess. Please, please tell me the weasel cunt still isn't worming her way in your brain."

Derek shook his low-hanging head, "No, Von, it's not her... I swear."

"Then what in fucking hell is this?" Siobhan demanded gently.

"Goddamn, it! I don't know... I'm just...I don't know. I'm fucking over it," he stated more harshly than he intended.

Siobhan's eyes went wide, and she shook her head at him, "No... no... just fucking no. That goddamn bitch isn't worth any of your fucking energy... stop giving it to her."

"I'm not trying to Von... fuck. You think I like being like this?" For the first time in a while, Derek was finally feeling emotion, but that emotion was anger.

"I'm just tired. I'm tired of hearing about her, I'm tired of dealing with questions every fucking day from people about *'What happened?' 'Did you hear what she's doing now?'* I'm tired of paying a fucking lawyer to deal with her... this," he gestured around him, "This was supposed to be fun. This was supposed to be my life...and someone is trying to take it away. Fuck I'm just tired... and bored....and...*pissed*." He looked down at his shaking hands. He clenched them tightly and looked back up at Siobhan, tears streaming down her fair face.

She tried to choke down her words to make them come out steady, "Please, Derek... don't do anything...stupid."

He paused to process her words then rolled the chair close to her, taking her hands in his, "Oh my god, Siobhan... no. I didn't mean that...I'm not thinking about anything like that."

He laid his forehead on her knee, "You know I fucking hate it when you cry."

A small chuckle came from Siobhan as she patted his head, "I'm sorry. I know."

Derek stood up and looked down at her. Even with her sitting on the table, he towered over her. Wrapping his arms around her he hugged her tightly, whispering, "I've told you before, never, ever apologize for your heart." He kissed her on the forehead, "Love ya, Von... I'll be okay."

Siobhan looked up at him, her green eyes drying, and she hopped off the table, "Back at you." She sighed and tousled his hair once again, "You need a haircut too."

Derek laughed at her and ran his fingers through his hair, smoothing it back again. "Off my back woman," he teased.

"C'mon...we've got work to do," she said as she playfully punched him in the arm.

Derek dove into his work, keeping the shop open until one a.m. as he did most nights. Besides he and Theo, there was one other artist with space in the studio and the trio could keep their schedules relatively full. Siobhan made sure each person had a least a twenty-minute break in between sessions and filled in dead space with walk-in clients. Because they had eight separate session rooms, when they were fully staffed, each artist could have two rooms apiece. After a sitting ended, Siobhan would sanitize the room and reset it for the next client assigned to that space. The studio ran like a well-oiled machine.

Theo locked the door after the final customer of the night left. He turned to Siobhan who was securing the cash drawer, "What do you say we grab Derek and force him into something completely terrible."

"Like?" she mused.

"I'm thinking beer and pool," he replied.

She gave Theo a half-grin, "That would be great... except, I'm pretty sure he would protest."

At that moment, Derek appeared from the small bathroom, just to the right of Siobhan's desk, "Who would protest what?"

Siobhan gave him a flat stare, sighing, "You— being social with your friends."

Derek ran his hand over his face and considered the offer. He strolled around the desk and put his hands on Siobhan's shoulders, "Von, I would do it for you."

She turned abruptly, "You're fucking with me, right?"

"No, not fucking with you," Derek raised his eyebrows, chuckling.

"Shit. Let's hurry before this asshole changes his mind," Theo laughed.

***

James Station was located on the same block as the tattoo shop, just three doors down and around the corner. The trio had begun hanging out there when the renovations to the studio were taking place, as the little neighborhood dive bar offered greasy and delicious culinary concoctions until the early hours of the morning. There was not much in the way of space, but seats for patrons could always be found.

The entirety of the bar consisted of about fifteen small square tables that were situated sporadically around the cozy space. There was an antique-looking bar at the front of the room with just enough area for one person behind it. A large assortment of bottles crowded the wall behind the bartender. There were two televisions in opposite corners of the room that only showed sports highlights and an old jukebox stood along the outside wall next to the one pool table the bar featured. James Station was a diamond in the rough and somewhere friends could always be found.

After claiming a table in the very corner of the room, Theo went to the bar, bringing back three beers.

"Dude. Finally," he said to Derek as he sat them down.

Derek only gave a slight smile.

Siobhan could see how uncomfortable Derek was but didn't want to show it. It was something she also noticed at the office and how he had become blandly transactional with customers. He was disinterested in everything, and it worried her. She waited for Theo to distract himself with a pretty girl with purple hair at the table behind them before she spoke.

She leaned close to Derek, "Look... I know you're faking this. You couldn't give a shit about being here...why don't you take off?"

Derek looked a little offended. Why would she want to get rid of him? After weeks of her and Theo's harassment, tonight, he finally relented. He really was trying to have a good time. Christ, was she ready to blow him off?

As if she read his mind, she responded quickly, "Reek... c'mon. I know you... I know that look. Just...don't do anything stupid."

Derek shook his head, "No. I told you I would come to hang out... so, I'm hanging."

About that time a couple of acquaintances strolled over and picked chairs to sit next to their table. Before long, there was a group of about ten sitting around two small tables laughing and sharing stories. Derek once again lost interest in the conversation and the overall noise. He stared off, scanned the crowds, and drank his beer absently. He continued to let his mind wander until someone caught his eye. Derek noticed her first, or so he thought. She and the man she was talking to, stood leaning against the bar. She swirled her drink absently as he spoke. Derek could see that she was tall and lean, and her dark blonde hair hung in loose ringlets down her slender back.

Derek watched her movements with purpose; she was mesmerizing. Every motion and every move seemed effortless yet deliberate. The gentleman she was speaking to must have been incredibly funny because she threw her head back several times in open laughter. Derek noticed every time she did, she gently touched the man's hand. Something about the touch seemed to electrify the man. Derek swore he saw the man shiver with each touch and laugh louder. He was snapped out of the world he shared with the two strangers by a familiar voice.

"Reek...hey," Siobhan nudged his arm.

"Yeah?" he answered without moving his eyes from the bar.

She stared at him for a moment, "What the hell are you looking at?"

Siobhan followed his stare across the room to the bar. She saw the beautiful, tall blonde woman touching the man's face.

She rolled her eyes, "Well, she's cute. But clearly with someone else." She flipped him on the ear as he stared off again, "Dude. Where are you?"

Derek took his eyes off the woman at the bar and looked at Siobhan, "I'm just..." He trailed off and looked back at where the woman was standing; she and her date were gone.

2

—·—

The image of the woman from the bar continued to burn for days in Derek's mind. She was beautiful; she was elegant in her movement; she was ethereal. Even after a week, he played that night over in his head. The way she held her hands. The movement her head made when she laughed. The manner in which she touched her companion's arm. The way the man seemed to shiver when she touched him. Derek imagined himself waiting for her at the bar. He saw himself falling into the depths of her eyes and living there. He blinked and the fantasy faded into mist and nearly forgotten memory.

He looked down at the sketch pad. The dragon twisted its neck back upon itself to lay its head on its own back. The scales were drawn lightly and expertly across its body. Smoke billowed around its delicately folded wings; the entire creature perched atop a golden Celtic knot egg. Derek didn't remember making as much progress on the custom piece that was on the paper and as he looked at the clock, an hour had passed.

The empty studio was getting darker by the minute as the sunset was slowly dropping behind the tall buildings. Derek decided to catch up on projects while they were closed for the day. He knew neither Theo nor Siobhan would be in, and he could have the quiet he yearned for. Theo was, for all intents and purposes, his adopted brother, and

Siobhan was his best friend, but their constant efforts to cheer him up made him want to strangle himself. No matter what he did or said, he couldn't convince them he was over the *weasel cunt* and that she wasn't even a blip on his radar. His world though, felt gray, and he was bored with it. Nothing seemed to excite him, not even his art. Numbness radiated around him and through him. He didn't know how to make them understand that the dark cloud around him was coming from the inside and was not caused by any external force.

He closed the sketchbook and threw his pencil in the desk drawer. Grabbing his keys, he made sure all the lights were out, set the alarm, and locked the front door behind him. He took a deep draw of the cool night air, and it was sharp in his lungs. He pulled his jacket around him and started the walk to his apartment. He moved with purpose keeping his head low and eyed the cars that occasionally rolled by on the crowded street. His tattoo shop was just one of many businesses on the busy thoroughfare. The neighborhood had been through several iterations and now it was an up-and-coming area with unique boutiques, bakeries, shops, restaurants, and bars.

Derek rounded a corner and ran into the end of a line of people, bringing him to an abrupt stop. One advantage of being almost six feet four inches tall was that he was able to see over almost anyone. He craned his neck and slowly eased his way around the line to find that it was not really a line at all; just a group of people smoking outside of what looked like one of the newly opened bars. He remembered seeing construction on the block but thought it was another craft bistro or bakery.

He slowed as he strode by to peer inside. Smooth, electronic music flowed out of the open door, and the dark expanse beyond was only lit with red and purple neon. He started to walk by but stopped suddenly, turned, and cruised by an inattentive doorman who was more interested in the tall brunette in front of him.

The air was cool inside the club, but Derek understood why there were so many people outside. The room was completely packed with bodies. To the right of the door was an expansive dance floor with throngs of people swaying to the hypnotic music. Derek could see low tables lining the edge of the room with plush red velvet sofas and chairs. Above the dance floor were two balconies that accommodated what he could only assume were VIP areas. He watched several men and women talking and pouring drinks on the left landing. On the right, he saw two women dancing very erotically for a single male patron.

He made his way to the giant black glass bar that took up almost the entire left side of the space. He found an empty bar stool, also covered in the same dark red velvet, and sat. The interior of the bar space held five drink masters and they seemed to move like a machine; never in each other's space.

A very tall and pale male bartender leaned in close to him and asked, "What can I get you?"

Without hesitation, Derek replied, "Whiskey, neat."

The blonde man nodded once and with expert hands quickly poured his drink and placed it in front of him. Derek handed him cash and took a pull from his glass. The whiskey was smooth and left very little of the familiar burn as it when down. He closed his eyes for just a moment to take in the feeling as the warmth worked its way to his soul. He listened to the sounds around him; the blurred chatter of conversations close by the clink of glasses as they were set on tables, and the reaching music from the deejay booth.

He allowed the sounds and smells and sights to wash over him as he tried to push the numbness away. He swirled the amber liquid slowly in his glass as he began to lift his eyes back up to the room. The hair on the back of his neck began to rise as he felt like he was being watched. He slowly cut his eyes to his right and noticed *her*.

She leaned close to speak into his ear, "No amount of sapience can be used to force emotional well-being. You have to desire peace and happiness." Her ringlets hung softly around her exquisite face.

Derek felt something like exhilaration as her breathy words touched his ear. He smiled at her and locked a gaze with the beautiful stranger's ice-blue eyes. He leaned into her and said, "Buddha or Nietzsche?"

She tossed her head back in a hearty laugh and her blood-red lips parted to show perfect snow-white teeth. She leaned back into him and said, "Daria."

Derek raised an eyebrow and asked, "Daria?"

Daria smiled again broadly as she plucked the cherry out of her drink and pulled it off the stem with her marble-like teeth. She chewed the fruit slowly as she stared at him. When she finished, she placed the stem back in her empty glass and raised her chin slightly at the blonde bartender. He immediately remade her drink and sat it in front of her. She touched Derek's hand softly, "My name...Daria."

A pulse, much like a small vibration from a TENS unit, started at her touch point and made its way up Derek's arm. He blinked and shook his head slightly, "I've seen you before."

"I know," Daria said as a matter of fact. She smiled again at him, this time a little more seductively, and ran a finger over his hand. The pulse, just slightly more intense this time climbed over him. "What is it you want?" she asked.

His head felt a little disconnected and he started feeling the beat of the music wash over him, "What do you mean? As in out of life?"

She shrugged her shoulders and sipped her drink, "Out of life, next month, next week...tonight."

Without hesitation, Derek answered, "I want to feel alive again... or at least feel...something."

Daria wove her fingers into his. The wave of pulsation moved steadily through his arm and into his head. The oscillation made him feel dizzy and euphoric. It felt like he was buzzing from ten drinks and high on the most in-vogue drug. He wanted her to envelop his entire body with hers. He wanted to feel her vibration all over him. He leaned closer to her, brushed a lock of her hair behind her ear, and breathed in her scent. She arched her back and pressed closer to him and purred. Looking down at her, his lips nearly touching hers.

Did her eyes get...paler?

Derek tried to shake the murkiness from his brain. He looked down as Daria removed her hand from his. As she did the vibration seemed to fade away and leave him completely. The fog and dullness began to fade, and he felt that he was sobering up after an all-night bender. He looked down into Daria's eyes and they seemed paler still. Was this real? He bent over and kissed her on the lips softly.

Daria pulled away gently and Derek noticed her chest pressing tight against her silky black crop top. She ran her finger over his lips and the gentle pulse rode its way through his skull. She turned away and with one finger, tugged on his belt loop in a gesture for him to follow her. Derek complied without hesitation, meandering behind her, and just avoided bumping into partygoers on the dance floor. Behind the stage where the deejay mixed the hypnotic and pulsating music, was a wooden door. Painted solid black like the wall, it blended almost perfectly.

Daria led Derek through the door and took an immediate right down a wide hall. The music was almost nonexistent even though he knew it blared just on the other side of the wall. They walked in silence for about thirty yards and came upon an elevator. Daria pushed the arrow up and turned to stare up at Derek.

"What do I call you?" she asked.

Derek blinked, licked his lips, and swallowed hard. His mouth was so dry. He looked down at her and a voice that he didn't realize was his said, "Whatever you choose."

Daria slid a sinuous arm out and brushed his face with her hand, "My choice, huh?'

Derek never noticed her icy eyes flaring with cold blue fire as she led him into the elevator.

They rose one floor and stepped off the lift. He followed Daria down a hallway with doors every twenty feet. Derek was trying to get his bearings. Where was he? He rubbed at his temple and shook his head. He felt as though he had too much cold medicine with too much beer.

"Where are we going?" he asked coherently.

Daria turned slowly to face him and ran another finger down his face. The electric charge sent gentle waves throughout his head and down his spine.

"Shhhh..." she soothed him, "I'll take care of you."

Daria turned around and opened a door to her left. Without looking, she slid her hand over the wall to turn on a dim lamp that sat on an adjacent table.

The room, which was more like a hotel space, was sparsely furnished with modern décor. A large king-sized bed took center stage. The headboard was tall and covered in the same blood-red velvet as the furniture in the club. The bed itself was fitted with black satin sheets and matching red velvet pillows. The lamp was the only light source in the room.

She led him to the bed as Derek struggled to stay in control of his mind and surroundings. He tried in vain to shake his head into clarity. As he did, Daria ran her hand under his shirt and placed her fingers over his heart. Her fingers felt hot and cold at the same time, but it was the waves of energy that made him weak in the knees. As if she knew he might fall over, she gently directed him to sit at the edge of the soft bed. He looked up at her, his eyes glazed and glassy. She smiled wide and looked down at him, her snow-white teeth sharp and glistening.

Daria reached behind herself and unzipped her short skirt and shook it to the floor as she shed her blouse. She stood in front of him voluptuous, inviting, and nude. Derek stared blankly at her.

She bent down and whispered to him, "Show me what you want."

And, with the smoothness of a serpent, she took his hands and slid across the bed with him.

Derek's brain was on fire and screamed at him fiercely. He knew there was something wrong, there was something not right with what was happening. Why couldn't he control himself? Sure, this girl was *exceptionally* attractive, but he had never been a one-night stand kind of guy. He didn't just bed a woman he just met in a bar. He felt like his motions were coerced but the more he fought them the more he was pulled toward her.

Derek, now lying on top of her, felt her firm breasts pressing against him.

He began to shake his head 'No. NO,' he thought, '*This isn't right...something isn't right*'.

Daria grabbed his head and kissed him hard. When she did a wave of energy surged through all of Derek's limbs. He was suddenly calm and warm; much like being in a cocoon. Daria ran her fingers under his shirt again and he assisted her in lifting the shirt over his head. He hovered over her, propped on his elbows as she relieved the rest of his body of its clothing.

Daria cooed in his ear as her hands explored his torso. He was well-built with a broad frame and ample muscle tone. She ran her fingers over his arms tracing each tattoo with her long nails.

"Do you want me, lover?" she breathed.

Derek licked his dry lips. While a distant voice in the back of his mind yelled about control and the need to wake himself out of this spell, the words that came out were a vacant "Yes."

He began to grind against her body, and she allowed him, wet with excitement.

3

— · —

Flashes of ecstasy and sweat and color rolled as an incoherent blur in his mind. He felt her body quiver and jerk beneath him. Her yells and cries of climax were like crashing thunder in his ears and her hair was soft clouds on his face. Her lips were wet and everywhere they touched he felt more soft pulses on his flesh. He ran his fingers from the nape of her neck to the small of her back as she climbed on top of him for one more smooth, rhythmic ride. A drunken haze clouded his mind. Time seemed to ebb and flow with the motion of their bodies...

Derek bolted upright in the bed.

Looking around the room, he recognized the lamp on his bedside table which was lit and overturned. He continued to gaze around his bedroom as if trying to re-familiarize himself with it. Pressing the heels of his hands into his eyes, he rubbed them hard.

Gathering his bearings, he searched for his phone. He discovered it lying on the floor as though it had been pushed off the bedside table and overturned. He checked the time: one p.m. He noticed he had several missed text messages from Theo and Siobhan and a voicemail. Listening to it, Siobhan told him that if he had not called her by twelve-thirty, she would be sending out a search party. At that moment, he heard a knock at the door.

Derek threw his legs over the bed and took notice that he was still fully dressed. Standing, his head swam but he staggered toward the door. Leaning heavily on the jamb, he opened it to find Siobhan on the other side holding a large cup with what he could only imagine was the life-giving nectar of hot coffee.

"Hey," he said hoarsely.

She rolled her eyes at him and shoved the cup in his hand, "Yep."

Walking past him, she let herself into his apartment. He shut the door and turned to face her, still leaning on the wall. He was glad it was there because it was the only way he knew it was his head spinning and not the room itself. Derek lifted the lid and sipped the dark liquid carefully.

Siobhan turned to get a good look before she railed on him, but as she did, she realized exactly how terrible he looked, "Reek. What's wrong with you? You look awful."

"Gee, thanks," he offered in retort as he headed to the sofa but, as he did, his legs buckled, and he crumbled to his knees.

"Oh, my God! Derek!" Siobhan yelled, rushing to help him stand.

Derek's head was swimming and he felt twisted inside and nauseous. He held out his arm as if to keep her from coming too close.

"Don't," he shook his head, "I'm fine."

He raised his head to look at her but felt as though he might pass out. Siobhan held out her hand in an offer to help him stand.

"Don't be stupid... let me help you," she demanded of him gently.

Derek finally accepted the offer, rose slowly, and allowed her to walk him to the end of the large, overfilled sofa. She no sooner turned to find him a blanket when he rolled off the couch and began to vomit on the floor. His painful heaving only stopped when he fainted.

Derek woke again to find himself comfortably placed back on his sofa, the fresh smell of disinfectant in the air. He was covered in the blanket from his bed and while he remained in his jeans from the night before, his shirt had been removed. He could hear the soft *swish, swish, swish* of the washing machine in the back closet of his apartment. Turning his head, he watched Siobhan sitting in the chair opposite him reading the most recent edition of *Tattoo Monthly*.

"Von," Derek tried to say strongly, but because his throat was on fire from the heaving and bile, came out as a whisper instead.

Siobhan lifted her head, looking at him with heavy concern, "Hey... feel any better?"

She didn't hold any judgment or hardness in her voice; it was just kind. She reached over and felt his head. Her hand felt soft and warm.

Derek cleared his throat quietly, "Yeah, I think so."

He noticed her clear green eyes beginning to glisten with tears, but just as fast as they appeared, he saw her blink them away by sheer will.

"You want to talk about what happened last night?" she asked.

Derek looked a little embarrassed, "I'm not sure *what* happened."

He saw a shadow of confusion cross Siobhan's face, "What I mean to say is, I've only got bits and pieces."

"Wow... You drank a lot. Which... isn't like you," Siobhan's voice was tinted with slight suspicion.

"No, I didn't!" Derek's voice was a little more defensive than it needed to be.

"Okay... I'm sorry, I wasn't..."

Derek cut through her apology, "No, I'm sorry. I didn't mean to snap. Von, I don't know what's wrong... But something is really fucking weird. I don't remember a lot about last night, but what I do know is that I only had one drink.... I swear."

The more he spoke the more he could hear panic rising in his own voice; all in the defense of his actions.

Kneeling by the sofa, Siobhan seemed to sense this too, "Hey, okay... You don't need to explain yourself... I've just never seen you act...well...hungover. That's all."

Derek threw the blanket off himself and made to stand off the sofa. As he did, he felt a little unstable and was forced to steady himself again.

"It's not a hangover!" he said, again with a little more force than he intended.

Siobhan looked up at him and, for the first time in the six years they had known each other, Derek could see the hurt and anger in her eyes that *he* had caused.

Standing from the couch, she grabbed her purse off the table. She uttered under her breath, "Just trying to help, dickhead," and walked out the door, slamming it in her wake.

Derek stared at the door. He immediately knew what he had done, and the shame filled him. He had never barked at her like that before. Sure, they had their own disagreements and their own arguments, but he had never treated her like she was a fool. What the hell was wrong with him? He knew he would have to apologize. He didn't think he could bear the thought of Siobhan being angry with him or worse; ashamed of him. But, chasing her out the door was not an option right at this moment. For one, he needed a shower but second, and most importantly, he needed to rest for just another moment. He felt the dizziness coming on again, although not as bad as before, and he was still a little queasy. What had happened last night?

Shuffling into the kitchen area, he noticed the large pot simmering on the stove. He lifted the lid and the warm and salty steam danced in his nose. Siobhan had made him homemade chicken soup. Derek felt more like an ass now than he had five minutes prior.

"Damn it," he whispered to the empty room as he found a bowl and served himself some of her magical brew.

An hour later, Derek, feeling a little more like himself, slid into the Jeep. He finished his bowl of soup and put the rest away for later, took a long, hot shower, and got dressed. He was not one hundred percent, but this would come close. He tried calling Siobhan twice, but she didn't answer; he knew he had really hurt her feelings. And every time he thought about it, his heart would ache. Siobhan was not particularly sensitive; she blew almost everyone off, allowing things to roll off her back. But Derek also knew that Siobhan was not close with a lot of people and the relationships she did have meant a lot to her.

Siobhan's family life could be called an American tragedy. She was the youngest of two children, her brother Mike just two years older. Their father had verbally and emotionally abused both the children from the jump. Siobhan would say that her father was an asshole when he was sober, but after he got a few drinks in him, he was the devil. The older Mike and Siobhan got, the more physical the abuse became. '*Spare the rod and spoil the child'* was his philosophy and he ruled the entire family with his fists. That was until he finally went to prison for the attempted murder of his wife, Siobhan, and Mike's mother. That was not to say that their mom was completely without her own faults. After Siobhan's father went to prison, her mother spiraled out of control. The stress of going from an abusive husband to a single parent took its toll on her and she began to drink heavily, which unfortunately turned into casual drug use. She moved Mike, Siobhan, and herself into her mother's house when the kids were in high school, but the move didn't seem to stabilize her, and she continued to spin out of control. Siobhan's grandmother begged her daughter to get help for years, but every time she fell off the wagon, it seemed her addictions only got worse. The drug use became obsessive until she was found, by Siobhan's grandmother, on the bathroom floor, dead from an overdose.

Siobhan's brother Mike became her rock. He joined the Army right out of high school and was determined to make a better life for himself and his sister. Because their mother was inattentive at best, Mike supported Siobhan financially as best he could. When their mother died, he paid for her funeral and made sure Siobhan had everything she needed. But tragedy struck again when on Mike's second tour of Afghanistan the convoy of medical supplies he was securing was hit by a roadside IED.

While he did survive the bombing, he was only one of three that did. This was especially difficult for Mike, and he fell into a deep depression. While home on leave, the despair he felt became overwhelming, and, in an effort to make the nightmares of that day end, Mike shot himself in the head. At the age of twenty-three, Siobhan was alone. Her only living relative was her father, and she had no use for him. She even changed her last name to further distance herself from the incarcerated felon.

Derek met Siobhan three years later while working at a telemarketing call center. It was the kind of job that provided the two things a person in their mid-twenties wanted: a decent income and a schedule that allowed for plenty of party time. They were assigned to the same training class and seemed to hit it off on day one. During breaks, they would talk ad nauseam about tattoos and music, which led to bigger life conversations. They quickly became close friends and started meeting up after work with their significant others for drinks and weekend camping trips.

After about two years of the daily grind, Derek had finally saved up enough money to move on to his real dream of owning his own tattoo shop. He had apprenticed for years on the weekends, and it was finally time to be on his own. Siobhan didn't hesitate to volunteer to help him, and his business partner Theo renovate the space they leased. She spent all her free time helping them paint walls, install new floors, and move furniture. She even helped Theo's girlfriend plan a small grand opening celebration. Her dedication to his dream didn't go unnoticed and when Theo went through a fairly nasty and public breakup with that same girlfriend, Derek offered Siobhan her receptionist job. And she didn't hesitate with her acceptance.

Where Siobhan was a loyal force for Derek, he became an anchor for her as well. While her professional life seemed in order, Siobhan's personal life was like a train wreck that no one could stop watching. In the six years of knowing each other, she had been in three relationships; all of which could have made any soap opera look like children's theater. When Derek and Siobhan met, she was in a relationship with a weightlifter named Nate who also worked at the same call center. The pair seemed to have a good connection with each other until Siobhan caught him having sex with another woman in their own bedroom.

Her second boyfriend, Joey, was a laborer who worked in the building across the street from Derek's shop. When the shop remodels were happening, Joey would come by to check the progress and then *"...head to the night job... "*. It didn't take long for Siobhan to find out that the *night job* meant stealing and striping cars for parts; at least that's what the police told her when they questioned her about his alibi after he was arrested. The last boyfriend was a little harder to get rid of and needed a little convincing from Derek and Theo to get lost.

She met Paul shortly after the breakup with Joey. Paul seemed like a nice guy, and he made Siobhan happy. He didn't have another girlfriend, an illegal hobby, or even a parking ticket. She always joked with Derek about how she was a *"loser magnet"*, so Paul seemed like a complete reset for her. Derek really liked Paul too and thought he was good for her. Paul was employed, friendly, and always seemed to be concerned about her well-being. In Paul, Siobhan thought she saw her future. But what none of them realized was that Paul had a dark side.

It began with small, off-handed comments about the kind of food she liked, how her martial arts interests weren't ladylike, and how much time she spent with Derek. Then after a few months, Paul's attitude and demeanor completely began to change. He started calling Siobhan constantly at work to make sure she was there. If she didn't answer the phone by the third ring or if it happened to go to the voicemail because she was on another line, it would infuriate Paul and he would show up to the tattoo shop in a rage. There were several occasions where Siobhan had to coax Paul out to the alley so he wouldn't be overheard berating her. Life with Paul continued to go downhill from there.

Siobhan did her best to keep everything hidden from Derek. While he was her closest friend, she never wanted to be a burden on him. She remembered Derek being frustrated with the public drama that Theo's previous girlfriend caused when they broke up and she didn't want that kind of attention. She spent most of her time in quiet embarrassment. What she didn't know though was that neither Derek nor Theo was blind to what was happening. Both men noticed how quiet Siobhan had gotten around the office. After the opening pleasantries, she kept to herself and didn't partake in the usual banter around the office. She also ran late to work at least twice a week, which was completely out of character for her. But it was the smaller details that Derek witnessed that disturbed him more than the issues with her attendance.

He noticed seemingly insignificant things such as when she began to wear her hair, clothes, and makeup differently and in ways he *knew*

she didn't like. There were bigger signs. One afternoon, she showed
up with some dark bruises on her arms and explained them away as a
"kickboxing class mishap". What she didn't know was that Derek had
spoken to her instructor the week before when he called to check on
her. He told Derek that she had not been to class in three weeks, and
he just wanted to make sure she was okay.

Still, Derek decided to wait to say anything to her. He thought
maybe she would come to her senses. He thought she would see her
father in Paul and make the right decision. Derek considered a con-
frontation with her about everything but was unsure how and when
to do it. Instead, he decided to go the passive-aggressive route and put
a ban on personal visitors to the office. He thought that would create
some space between Siobhan and Paul and give her at least eight hours,
or more, of respite every day.

His plan was short-lived because, after just two weeks of the new
house rule, he came out of a session room to find the reception area
vacant. After a quick look outside, he saw Paul talking to Siobhan
in his car, and from the look of his body language, Paul was angry.
Siobhan got out of the car, shut the door, and watched him drive
away. Derek kept an eye on her for five minutes standing outside of
the tattoo shop and crying. He waited until she pulled herself together
then he disappeared back to his office before she could reenter and
catch him. Derek's patience was growing thin, and he questioned how
much more *she* could take. He finally made the choice to intervene and
bring his concerns directly to her. He purposefully chose a day that
had the least number of clients and waited until she got settled before
he knelt beside her.

"Von, can we talk?" he asked softly.

But before she could respond, Paul walked in the door. Siobhan
suddenly busied herself tidying her desk area and turned her back on

Derek. Paul, who was not able to see Derek from the front of the tall desk, came around the counter and jerked Siobhan by the arm. She jumped with a start out of her chair as Derek popped up next to her.

The sudden appearance of Derek clearly shocked Paul as he released Siobhan's arm almost immediately. All Derek could think was that his suspicions were right, and it made his blood boil. Before he could stop himself, Derek had Paul against the door, cursing and beating him out of his shop.

"You son of a bitch!" Derek bellowed as he shoved Paul by the shirt collar against the frame of the door. "You mother fucker! You laid hands on her!? What else did you do!?"

"Derek! No!" Siobhan yelled as Theo came running around the corner to see what the commotion was about. He tried to get between Derek and Paul, but Derek's height gave him a clear advantage and he was able to block Theo.

Derek shoved Paul's back against the frame again, his eyes wild with fury, "You get out of my shop, you fucking piece of shit! Don't you dare show yourself here ever again!"

"Is that what *you* want?" Paul choked and smiled weakly at Siobhan.

Her eyes were filled with fear, but Siobhan cleared her throat and whispered, "Yes."

Derek shoved Paul through the front door with force as Siobhan collapsed into Theo's arms. By this point in the relationship, Siobhan and Paul were practically living together. So, when it came time to head home for the night, Derek knew he had to make sure she was going to be safe. He convinced Siobhan to come to his apartment for a while so they could talk; promising he and Theo would make sure Paul removed his stuff from her apartment the next day. Derek just wanted to take her mind off everything and give her some peace.

He ordered take-out, and they watched movies and played cards until the wee hours of the morning. When she finally decided to open herself up and tell him everything that happened, he held on to her as she cried herself to sleep in his arms. His heart ached for her, and he wanted to take all the pain Paul had caused away, but he knew she would have to heal herself. He knew guys like Paul; he *hated* guys like Paul and underneath it all, Derek was disappointed in himself that he didn't recognize the signals and step in before.

Now, Derek sat in his Jeep and thought again about the hurt Paul had caused Siobhan. Although she told him what had happened between them, Derek knew the story was probably much worse. He felt it was better that he may not know all the details because he didn't feel a stay in the county jail was the best use of his time. After that breakup, Siobhan made a commitment to herself to never live with that fear again. She finished earning her black belt in Taekwondo and had begun studying Krav Maga. She had gone back to her kickboxing and used it most of the time as a stress relief activity. Derek knew today this was, most likely, where he could find her and decided he would check her gym first.

He would never forget the way she jumped when Paul grabbed her that day in the studio. Derek didn't have a family and had been an orphan. Theo and Siobhan meant the world to him; they *were* his family. He would never forgive himself for causing her any pain. Had they argued over the years? Of course. What friends never argue? But he had hurt her this time and that was different.

The stop at her gym was a bust as Siobhan had left about forty-five minutes before he arrived. Derek made one last, quick stop for a peace offering and headed to her apartment. He parked next to her truck and set out for the landing. He noticed one of her elderly neighbors leaving and realized he wouldn't need Siobhan to ring him in the building. Holding the door for the stooping, silver-haired woman, Derek slipped in behind her. Because of his long legs, he easily took the stairs two at a time. Once he reached the third-floor landing and her door, he knocked softly. After a short pause, which he knew was Siobhan looking through the peephole and probably deciding whether to let him in or not, he heard the click and slide of both locks.

Siobhan's obscured face peeked around the door.

"Hey," she said quietly.

"Hey... can I come in?" Derek asked. Siobhan nodded and opened the door wide to allow him to pass.

As he stepped over the threshold, she noticed the brown bag he was carrying.

"What's that?" she asked.

A sweet smile spread across his handsome face, "My apology."

He handed her the small bag and watched a soft smile appear on hers, "Mint chip. Still your favorite, right?"

Siobhan nodded, putting the package in the freezer before turning to face him.

Derek took a deep breath, "Von, I'm sorry.... I don't know what my fucking problem was. I didn't mean to yell at you."

He stretched his arms out to offer a hug, "Forgive me?"

Siobhan eyed him with mock suspicion and leaned into his embrace, resting her forehead on his chest, "I guess."

"I really *am* sorry," he whispered in her ear before kissing her on the top of her head.

"I know," she whispered back, pulling away. "Now, you wanna talk about what happened last night?"

Derek sighed, walking over to her small kitchen table, before sitting in a chair, "I don't know...but I need help, Von."

"Start from the beginning."

Derek told her everything from the time he left the studio, what he could remember of his encounter with Daria, then waking in his own bed with no memory of how he got home.

Siobhan stared at him, dumbfounded, "So, this Daria, is the same woman we saw at the bar the other night? You're sure?"

Derek nodded, "Positive."

"And you're absolutely sure you only had that one drink?" she asked.

He looked her directly in the eyes, "Von, I swear to you I only had one drink."

Siobhan chewed on her lip, thinking a moment before she spoke again, "I mean, it's not common, but certainly not unheard of that a man gets roofied... could that be what happened?"

Derek shrugged, "I don't know... I really don't think so though. I watched the bartender pour my drink. And the more I think about it...since it's all I've been able to do today... I can remember *some* stuff that happened. In flashes...and I know she didn't touch my drink."

"What *can* you remember?" Siobhan asked.

"What it felt like when she touched me," he began, "It was like every time she did it was...a jolt."

"What do you mean a jolt?"

Derek stood and began to pace around the room, "Like a shock of electricity...a jolt. Nothing that hurt... just more of a vibration."

His head began to pound like a drum, and he rubbed his temples between his hands, "My head felt foggy after that."

Siobhan studied him carefully, noticing him become more uncomfortable with pain. "So, she what? Touches you and you get drunk?" she asked. "The aspirin is next to the sink."

Derek reached over, grabbing the bottle of white pills. Popping the lid open, he juggled out two and said, "No. I mean, like every time she touched me...it was..."

He threw his head back with a mouth full of water and swallowed hard. A sudden flash of memory came to him, "...every time she kissed me too. Almost like," he searched for the word, "A poison."

Siobhan looked a little incredulous and for a short moment, she thought he had actually lost his mind. But remembering that Derek was the most dependable, honest person she had ever met, she knew he had to be recalling the night in the truest way he could. She believed everything he was telling her although she also the thought crossed her mind that he may not have been choosing the correct words to describe how he felt at the moment. Nevertheless, she was determined to help him figure it out.

"Okay... let's start over. You meet in the bar... you order a drink then she approaches you. You two start talking, and she flirts a little, touching your arm?" She said, replaying the story again.

Derek nodded in agreement then stopped, "No. My hand."

"Okay, your hand. And that is when you feel this shock?" she asked.

He again nodded his agreement.

Continuing, she said, "Your head gets cloudy...like you've been drinking a lot."

His head was still nodding as he closed his eyes to concentrate on the memories that seemed to elude him.

"The pair of you continue to talk and she's still making skin contact with you. What did you talk about?" Siobhan asked.

He was desperate to remember the events of the night before. He focused on all the sensations he could find in his memory: the sound of the deejay, the smell of the room, and the taste of his drink. He slowly sat on the floor at Siobhan's feet, head still nodding softly. Derek's motions became rhythmic as he seemingly placed himself in a soft trance.

"Life... numbness... desire," he said quietly.

She considered his answer and waited a moment before asking her next question, "What about life? Do you mean your life?"

"*I want to feel alive again,*" Derek quoted himself as he continued to nod his head and now rock his body. The motion calmed his anxiety and helped open his mind a little more.

Siobhan was physically shocked by his admission. She was glad that his eyes were still closed because she didn't want him to see the tears that were starting to well in hers again. She knew that the breakup with the weasel cunt was hard on him, even if he didn't want to admit it to himself. Siobhan knew he was glad to be rid of her when she left because she finally saw him laugh with pure joy afterward. But when the weasel cunt tried to take away his dream; that's the moment when his heart froze.

Siobhan steadied her voice. "Okay, you talk about life. She's touching your hand. Then...?" she guided him through his self-meditative state.

"I kissed her," Derek opened his eyes slowly and his nodding stopped. "I don't know why I kissed her. I didn't want to, I felt like...I had to." His brow furrowed in confusion.

He looked up at Siobhan and found her round green eyes looking back at him; they were gentle and understanding. He knew he was looking at one of the only people on the earth he could trust with his life.

"I remember everything."

Derek sat on the kitchen floor in silence, the flood of memories rushing over him like waves crashing to shore. He remembered being led through the dance floor of the club and into an elevator. He recalled her leading him into the room with the bed and the seduction that followed. He realized that he both enjoyed it and was repulsed by it. He then journeyed through his recollection of what happened afterward.

As he lay naked and paralyzed on the bed, Daria redressed herself, turning to smile down upon him. She leaned closer and whispered in his ear, "I'm so sorry darling... I may have had to feast upon you a little too much tonight. You were *so* hard to control. I do hope you enjoyed yourself; I'm sure we'll do it again sometime...tonight was fun."

Her voice was different this time. It was no longer sweet or innocent but measured and dangerous. There was a deeper meaning to her words, something he couldn't understand. She kissed him on the cheek, making his right arm convulse. He saw her eyes were now a deep midnight blue.

There was a soft knock at the door and the blonde bartender entered. Derek couldn't hear what they were saying, but soon the bartender gathered his clothing off the floor and began redressing him. The blonde man was someone of immeasurable strength as he flipped Derek back and forth on the bed like a rag doll. He then hoisted Derek over his shoulders in a fireman's carry and set off with him out of the room. The blonde man walked with Derek down the rest of the hallway to a stairwell, continuing down with ease.

When they reached the bottom, the man pulled open the fire door to a dark sedan waiting in the alley. He laid Derek a little too roughly on the back seat and shut the door. He walked around to the driver's side, getting behind the wheel. Derek knew he wasn't very far from his apartment. Three, or four blocks? Because the blonde man laid him facing up, he could see out of the darkened windows of the car. He wished he could see the color of the sky. It must be close to midnight.

The car came to a stop and the blonde man opened the back-seat door and pulled Derek by his ankles. He again threw Derek over his shoulders and made his way to the apartment. He used Derek's keys to gain access and made his way with him to the bedroom. As the blonde man turned to place Derek on the bed, he knocked over the bedside lamp. He threw Derek's phone and keys on the floor, leaving the apartment.

"I remember it all," Derek said again softly after he retold the entire story.

Siobhan stared in shock at him, whispering, "Oh my god."

Awe and confusion rattled her brain at his recall of the rest of the evening. Another emotion was beginning to rise in her though, and that was anger. She slid out of her chair to sit next to him on the floor. Derek's face was blank of all expression but turned to her as she did. She hesitantly moved closer to him and let him rest his head on her shoulder.

4

Candlelight flickered sporadically in the darkness. Daria, nude, laid wantonly on the large bed, her cold blue eyes fixated on the small door in front of her. The gurgling sounds were like an erotic mix of music and lust in her ears. The door she stared down finally made a soft click and opened slowly. Alexis stood naked and fully erect in the doorway, his astoundingly fit body backlit by more candles.

Daria purred softly at his presence, "Is it done, lover?"

"It is," Alexis said smiling broadly, showing his own marble-white teeth. He crossed the room, sliding next to her on the smooth black sheets. "Are you ready my beloved?"

"Yesss," Daria continued to purr as her eyes rolled back into her head. "This child will be the beginning of our new destiny. We will finally put our kind where they belong...as the new head of the Hidden. We will have a new Order. And you and I, my love, will be the new ruling family."

Alexis kissed her with unabashed passion as he placed himself inside her.

5

— · —

Siobhan and Derek agreed it probably wasn't safe for him to stay at his apartment for the next few nights. Knowing there were strangers that knew where he lived and had already gained access to his home was unsettling for them both. He wasn't scared by any means but agreed with Siobhan that it was probably best to lay low somewhere else for a bit. Siobhan had a pull-out sofa and an extra bathroom, so it was the obvious first choice. Other than the temporary living arrangement, his and her routines wouldn't change.

On the third afternoon of arriving at the tattoo studio together, Theo was already inside. He stood at the coffee station dumping black grounds into a filter when they walked in.

Turning toward them, he smiled, "Good morning! I'm making coffee."

Siobhan winced, "Ew. I've already eaten... and it's twelve-thirty."

"Me too," Derek laughed.

Theo mused, "Curious..."

"What is?" Derek asked as he began turning on all the lights and started his computer in the next room.

"That this is the third day that you and Von have come in together... something I should know?" Theo grinned slyly, raising an eyebrow.

"Classy," Siobhan said pointedly back at him.

"No, Theo… Nothing to know… my apartment is just being fumigated," Derek lied dryly.

"Why wouldn't you stay at my pad?" Theo feigned hurt. "Am I not hot enough for you anymore?"

Derek turned sharply with quick fury in his eyes to deliver a piercing retort at his friend, but Siobhan cut him off, "No, Theo… it's that I make better coffee."

Siobhan gave Derek a look of silent confusion.

"Oh, ouch," Theo laughed and walked out of the reception area and back into his office.

Standing close to Derek, Siobhan whispered, "You haven't told him?"

Derek shook his head.

"He's your best friend… Any reason why?" she asked.

Derek looked over her head to make sure Theo was out of earshot, "Von, what exactly should I say? *Hey man, I'm going to hang out at Siobhan's for a few days while she helps me figure out this weird witch situation, I got myself into'*… C'mon…be serious."

Siobhan immediately shook her head and said, "No, not a witch."

"What?" Derek asked incredulously.

A look of excitement washed over her, "Not witch, Reek. You don't have a witch situation…but now I know who you should talk to!"

***

The afternoon and evening couldn't have gone by fast enough for Siobhan. She called, arranging a meeting that night with someone she thought might be able to help them. As they climbed into his Jeep, she could barely contain her anxiety. She gave him an address and they headed out of downtown to the picturesque Lair Hill neighborhood.

Water Street was lined with beautiful Victorian homes. Its picturesque scenery gave Portland its recognizable charm. Of all the gorgeous houses that had seen many families through the years, it was a small one on an unassuming corner they were the most interested in. The house was three stories with access to both the basement and main level street side. It was pale green in color and its trim was a darker shade of emerald. The small front yard was tidy yet wildly landscaped with plants of all colors and textures. A tall wooden privacy fence marked the property's backyard.

Putting the vehicle in park, Derek stared at the house, "Are you sure about this? I mean, this woman thinks she's a witch."

"Keep an open mind. And she is a witch... by definition," Siobhan said.

"*By definition*? What the hell does that mean?" he smirked.

Siobhan sighed in desperation, "Derek...just give her a chance. Julia is a really great woman... I think you'll like her. But more to the point, she studies weird stuff. I really think she'll be able to help you."

"Okay... But Von, I swear if I smell patchouli..."

Siobhan rolled her eyes at him, laughing, "Get out of the damn car."

As they made their way up the wooden stairs to the front door, Siobhan could see three stained glass windows: one above a large window to the left of the door, one over the doorway, and the third above the large window to the right of the door. They were beautiful panes of cobalt blue and warm oranges that surrounded a single pane of clear glass. Within each pane of clear glass held a white piece that represented the phases of the moon; moving from left to right, waxing, full, waning. Warm lights poured onto the porch through the spectacular pieces as Siobhan rang the doorbell.

Muffled steps came closer to the door and the click was soft as it opened. A thin woman many years older than the pair of them appeared from behind it. Her hair was dark, but lighter grey strands had begun to show around her temples. She wore a long burgundy skirt made of thin material and a black sweater. She was barefoot and carrying a kitchen towel in her hands.

A warm smile spread across her friendly face as she recognized Siobhan.

"Siobhan! Oh, my girl, how are you?" the greying woman reached out her arms to hug her. As she did, a soft scowl formed on her brow, "Oh. You carry a burden."

She looked over at Derek, taking his hand, "As do you, child... No more. Both of you please come in."

The living area was quite large and lit brightly with white candles on almost every flat surface. Older, comfortable-looking furniture was neatly arranged facing each other which Derek assumed was to encourage conversation.

As he took in the surroundings, Siobhan spoke an introduction for him, "Julia, thank you so much for seeing us. This is my friend Derek... Derek, this is Julia Silver. She's a..." Siobhan looked at Julia for approval which the woman quietly granted, "...the witch I told you about."

Derek looked at both women in disbelief, "You can't be serious? Like a real witch?"

Julia motioned for them to sit, smiling warmly at him, "Yes child... all my life. As is every descendant in my family line...women and men, alike."

Derek looked from Siobhan to Julia and back again, disbelief still heavy, "Von, I think I've had my fill of spell work for a lifetime."

She looked at him with desperation in her eyes, "I know Derek... but I really think Julia can help. We don't know why this happened or what we're even dealing with... Please, just listen."

"Her concern for you is honest and true, child. I understand that you have been a victim..." Julia began, but Derek immediately cut her short.

"Victim? I'm not a victim of anything," he defended boldly.

"No?" Julia eyed him, "May I then ask a favor of you?"

Derek looked at her suspiciously then at Siobhan, who nodded encouragingly. He granted his consent with reluctance.

Standing from her seat, Julia came closer to where Derek sat. She knelt down in front of him and said softly, "I'm going to place my hands upon your head, child. I need you to relax and close your eyes. Think only of the reason this girl has brought you to me."

"Vulcan mind meld?" Derek joked with a raised eyebrow.

Julia smiled sweetly, "Of sorts."

Derek was taken aback but nodded his approval, closed his eyes, and did as he was asked. He thought only of the memories of Daria. Julia's hands were cool and soft on his face, and she rested them there for several minutes until she let out a blood-curdling scream that startled his eyes open again.

"Julia!" Siobhan yelled as she jumped from her chair to catch the woman before she collapsed to the floor.

Julia looked up at both of them staring down at her, "I'm alright, child. I'm alright."

She allowed Derek and Siobhan to help her back to a chair and after a moment of catching her breath, she looked at Siobhan, "You were right to bring him here."

"What is it, Julia?" Siobhan asked quietly.

"Something I haven't seen in a long-time child...many, many years in fact. I thought they had all been run out of Portland but looks like they've made their way back. Evil, foul, unholy. I'll have to call in the Order... they can't be allowed to roam the streets unchecked." Julia spoke to the pair of them, her voice hard and determined.

"What? What is it?" Derek's voice was just as forceful.

Julia turned, looking Derek directly in his eyes, "You, my child, have been the desire of a succubus."

Siobhan and Derek stared at her for a moment.

"A...what?" They chimed together.

Julia folded her hands in her lap and took a deep breath, "A succubus. They're inhuman creatures that feed upon the life force of others... some call them and confuse them with demons. They're closely related but they aren't true demons."

Derek and Siobhan continued to stare with disbelief. A long pause fell between the three for a moment before Derek broke the silence, "You're fucking with me now. This isn't real."

His tone seemed to stun Siobhan out of a stupor, and she hissed her disapproval at him, "Derek! Be respectful."

Julia gave a soft chuckle, "It's okay Siobhan, don't chide him. Normally, I wouldn't discuss such things so openly with people of the Known. But your friend has been victimized by such a vile creature and I don't think this is a time for self-serving nuance."

She rose from where she was sitting, "Let me make us some tea."

Ten minutes later, the trio sat with mugs of freshly brewed, warm mint-chamomile tea in their hands. Julia took a delicate sip from her cup before speaking again.

"Let me start from the beginning. All beings on this earth live within two *worlds* if you will. There's what my kind call the Known, which encompasses everything you can see around you. This is everyday life... your grocery store, your mechanic, your home. Then," she took another sip, "There is the Hidden. This is where people like me can see and interact within a different realm if you will... in this world dwells all sorts of other human-like creatures that people like me have been charged with keeping out of the way of people like you, *Normalem*."

"People like us?" Derek asked.

Julia smiled sweetly, "Yes, my child... people like you. Average, everyday, *normal* people. Imagine the chaos that would be created if everyone knew of the Hidden World. An actual, physical place filled with witches, fae folk, vampires, ghosts, elementals, and succubae. Normalem already fills their children's heads with lesson-giving folktales about the residents of the Hidden to scare them into desired behaviors... imagine what would happen if they knew most of those stories were true."

"Chaos," Siobhan said flatly.

"In the most extreme child... but we work together to keep interaction in the Known to a minimum," Julia sat her empty mug on the table next to her.

"Work with... whom?" Siobhan asked.

"Within the Hidden, there is a governing body, The Order. It works to keep what needs to stay hidden away from Normalem, creates laws to govern our world, and punishes those that desire to undermine that delicate balance. In the Hidden, the residents are all variations of light and dark. And for the most part, we attempt to coexist peacefully... there are exceptions, of course, like..."

Derek's somber voice cut across Julia's, "... a Succubus."

Julia nodded, continuing, "Yes, my child...the Succubae. They feed and consume at their own will... they don't answer to any governing body or subset. They live by no code but their own and they hold all human life in ill regard unless it pertains to a food source. Even a vampire has morals," Julia said this last statement more to herself than to anyone else.

"You said you would have to tell The Order... what will they do?" Siobhan asked as her mind swam with questions.

"I'm unsure," she answered slowly. "I suppose to attempt to drive them out of Portland. Succubae can't be allowed to run rogue and unchecked through a city."

Julia gave a look of utter disgust.

Derek, who had become unusually still cleared his throat and asked quietly, "You said she fed on me. ..I need to know more."

"Child.... I've seen it in your head.... I think you remember enough," Julia countered.

"No, I don't... I need to know everything," Derek shook through clenched teeth.

Julia considered him for a moment. She rose, walking over to a large bookshelf behind Derek's seat. From there she pulled an old-looking book bound in dark, heavy leather. She returned to her position across from him and began flipping through its thick parchment pages. When she found what she was looking for she turned the book to face Derek and Siobhan. Siobhan took the book in her lap and began to skim over its pages.

Julia sighed heavily, "Most humans think of a Succubae as a female demon... this is not *exactly* accurate. The word indicates the race as a whole and the female gender of that race. They are indeed related to demons in a strict sense...they're distant cousins, even though most true demons won't admit it. Demons look at them as half-bred abominations. Much like true demons, they're vile, live to manipulate others, and have otherworldly abilities, but this is where the similarities end. Because they are part human, they have all the desires and needs that we do. They're always paired with a mate, an Incubus, and will form nests with other mated pairs."

"The bartender," Derek interjected. "How big is a nest?"

"It says here, as many as twenty," Siobhan answered.

Derek glanced over at the book to see an ancient drawing of a wild-haired, bare-breasted woman sitting upon a sleeping man, her icy white teeth in a position to bite his bared chest. Derek shuttered at the image as memory flashes of Daria's marble mouth flooded over him.

"That number is an extreme amount," Julia interjected. "Succubae aren't known for their tolerance of too many of their own species in one location. They don't have a strong governing structure like others in the Hidden. Most of us have our own elders we answer to... Witches have a coven counsel, Vampires, Fae, and the Elven have royal courts. At best, a nest of Succubae will have one or two alpha-type pairs. Although the Werewolves would be offended, I used their terminology to describe such offensive creatures," Julia chuckled softly.

Derek and Siobhan stared at the pages in front of them. It was surreal and impossible to think that all of what she was saying could be and was real. Vampires? Elves? She couldn't be serious, but she was. What she was saying pushed them well beyond information overload. They weren't talking about a Tolkien novel; this was real life and much more dangerous. How were they going to fight something like this? They couldn't exactly go to the police and report that Derek had been assaulted...by a *succubus*. It sounded crazy.

"Julia, please, how do they feed?" Derek tried to remain polite, but the desperation in his voice was beginning to break through.

"Yes, my child, I'm getting there...I'm sorry," she apologized. "Once a Succubus has her eyes set on someone, you for instance child, she uses her *diti'litro* to ease her prey into submission."

"Dilit...what?" Derek asked.

Siobhan began reading from the large book she still held on her lap, *"'The Succubae uses diti'litro, a type of electrified venom, to control her prey. This is administered by skin contact by the control of the Succubus. The diti'litro can cause a range of effects, depending on the dosage afflicted upon the prey, from euphoria to nausea to...'"* Siobhan stopped suddenly.

"What?" Derek demanded.

She swallowed hard and her throat had become suddenly dry.

"Death, child. She can, and will, kill." Julia interjected again, continuing, "After she has you soft and controllable, she can get into your mind and find out what your desires are, sexually. You see, she feeds off life energy, in particular the energy that is exuded and released during the Great Rite. She has the ability to take as little or as much as she wants. If she is hungry enough or greedy enough, she can take all of your life force... causing death."

Derek's head dropped into his hands, and he rubbed his face. He was exhausted and overwhelmed, "So, what you're saying is that I'm lucky I escaped with my life."

"No, my child, you haven't escaped anything. I've seen inside you... I know her intent. When she finds out you have survived, she will want more. I felt how much diti'litro she used on you... it was more than enough to kill. But you lived and she won't want you to... she *can't* allow you to now. Once you've come back to full strength, she will need all of your life force," Julia warned.

"Now what? What more could there be?" his voice was filled with anger and exhaustion.

"Because" Julia's voice became more soothing and motherly, "of the Chirion. She will need your life force to complete her task. And you will be seen as a threat...she can't allow you to live, and she *will* enjoy the hunt."

"Oh, God!" Siobhan gasped and Derek's head snapped in her direction.

"What?" he demanded.

"Child... A Chirion is a child of an Incubus and Succubus," Siobhan's voice shook. Derek looked around wildly at Julia.

"What do you mean a child? That bitch was pregnant?" Derek fired at Julia.

"She is *now* my child."

Derek's head began to swim, and he felt sick to his stomach again. The more he thought about it the more he wanted to run instead, he stood and began to pace around the room. He had to remain calm and keep a cool head.

He needed clarification because maybe, just maybe he didn't understand her correctly, "So, you're saying that I knocked this Succubus up? And this *Chirion*, is my fault?"

"You misunderstand me, child. None of this is your fault...she knew exactly what she was doing. And you didn't impregnate her directly, but she did use you to make herself that way. You see, she collected the seed from you, but it was the Incubus that impregnated her. Succubae and Incubae can't reproduce themselves, they need human seed. So, she collects it, he devours it, and implants it into her. They are incredibly fertile creatures and can produce a live Chirion within a few weeks," Julia explained calmly.

"That's disgusting," Siobhan stated emphatically.

"Very," Julia agreed.

Siobhan closed the book on her lap, handing it back to Julia. She walked over to where Derek was crouching on the floor, his head bent. She stooped close to him and placed her arm around his broad shoulders.

"It's okay... we will figure this out," she whispered to him. She looked up at Julia, "Okay. What do we do? Because I'll be damned if this bitch is getting him.... She's caused enough pain."

Siobhan began trembling with anger, "I'll kill her myself if I have to."

Julia's face hardened, "I believe you could. And I will help you, child, in any way I can. First, I must contact the Order. They won't be happy about this Succubae reproducing without the consent of the human."

Derek began laughing with exasperation and desperation, "You mean there are people who *want* this?"

"You would be surprised, my child," Julia turned back to Siobhan and walked into a small pantry just off the dining room, "Let me give him something to clear his body of the venom."

She returned a few minutes later with a black velvet bag tied with black ribbon and handed it to Siobhan, "Boil one teaspoon of this in water twice a day for three days and have him drink it...you might add some honey, it can be bitter."

She directed her next words at Derek who had just stood from his crouched state on the floor, "It'll stop that headache and the sickness."

Siobhan took the bag and she and Derek headed for the door, "We appreciate everything, Julia. You will call me?"

"As soon as I hear back from the Order," she assured.

"Derek, my child," she added with a warning, and he turned to face her, "Please, stay calm and out of trouble... this can be corrected. Don't let her find out where you are if you can. If she does, she will certainly come for you."

Derek nodded, "Thank you, Julia."

The door clicked softly behind them.

***

Water and herbs boiled ferociously in the kettle and just before the steam began to whistle, Siobhan removed it from the heat, pouring it into a large cup. She leaned down and smelled the steam rolling off the top; it smelled a lot like fresh-cut grass. She took the plastic bear from the counter and flipped the lid on its head. The amber liquid melted almost instantly in the hot brew as she stirred.

Derek hadn't moved from the end of the sofa after returning from his shower. His hair still damp, and dressed in tee-shirt and sweatpants, he sat motionlessly and stared into nothing. He played the last four days over and over in his mind. How had his life taken such an abrupt turn? A few days ago, he was just numb from life but still going through the motions, now he was hiding out in his best friend's apartment trying to figure out his next move to keep living. And he was a sperm donor for a monster's baby... life was great. He looked up just in time to see Siobhan handing him a cup of what looked to be lawn clippings. His nose curled at the scent.

"I added some honey. Hopefully, it'll taste better than it smells," she offered.

"Bottoms up," he said as he sipped cautiously. It wasn't *bad*, but it certainly wasn't going to win any awards. He was thankful the honey covered what he knew instinctively to be the worst of the flavor.

Siobhan sat in a small rocker across from him and he could see she wanted to talk but he didn't think he had any more energy to give. He continued sipping the tea until it was cool enough for him to gulp. He felt like a kid who had to take his medicine before he could have a treat, but this treat was not anything sweet to eat, just the possible relief from the pounding in his brain.

She cleared her throat, smiling softly at him; her green eyes shone warmly. "What was the name of that bar?" she asked.

Derek sat his empty cup on a side table and nodded his head, "Yeah, Riot... over on Morris."

He began to eye her suspiciously, "Why?"

She took a deep breath, "I'm going over there."

"Oh, hell no!" Derek said loudly.

"Reek just hear me...." she said defensibly.

"I said NO!" He raised his voice louder, thundering on, "There is no fucking way I'm letting you go over there."

"You need to listen to me..." she said firmly, her voice meeting his.

"I'm not hearing this... That's a stupid idea, and I won't let you do it." Derek's face became red with fury, and he stood over her, "She almost killed me. ME! What do you think she'll do to you? Huh?"

Siobhan stood to meet him. While she was only tall enough to come to the middle of his chest, she pulled herself to her full height, standing her ground.

"She won't do anything to me! She can't. Her venom won't affect me, it only works on men. And I'm not afraid of her," she railed on. "I also won't sit by and wait for her to hunt you down. If she wants a fight, I'll give her one. I want *her* to be the one running, not you!"

Derek took a small step back from her. In all the years he had known her, he had never once seen Siobhan as angry as she was right now, and he had also never seen her as strong or self-assured. He knew that he would never be able to talk her out of going, but maybe he could convince her that it would be safer if they stayed together.

"Okay. Okay, I get it," he said more calmly and raised his hands in surrender. "I know you're pissed. But Von, please let's think about this. If you go over there and by some chance you find her and you do get hurt, I'm not going to recover from that. Let me at least be your backup."

"Derek, that is the last place you need to be... you heard what Julia said," she retorted.

"I did. But this is also my life and my problem. I can't sit by and wait for some bogeywoman to come out of the shadows. I say let's go get her together," Derek grinned just a little, "Tomorrow."

6

—— ◦ ——

The spring Portland rain beat heavily on the third-story window and the gusting wind played a low throb against the building. The dark gray sky gave the illusion of early morning in the way the shadows cast on the carpeted floor. Siobhan stretched slowly under the intimate warmth of her blankets, reaching out to check the time on her phone; ten minutes before twelve.

It was no surprise to her that she had slept most of the day since her plans with Derek had run well into the early morning. They'd agreed to wait for a call from Julia, but they would also not stand by and be threatened. Whatever plan the Order was going to concoct, they wanted to be involved. It seemed noble; it could be insane, and it was terrifying.

Just as she threw the covers back to remove herself from her cozy cocoon, a faint buzzing rose from her phone. She answered it immediately when she saw Julia's name appear on the screen.

"Julia," she said quickly.

"Yes, child," Julia's honeyed voice responded.

Siobhan quickly made her way out of her bedroom and into the living room where Derek slept. She gave his foot a firm pull as she said, "What did you find out? What did the Order say?"

Derek was immediately awake. He sat up and listened intently as he ran his fingers through his hair. Before Julia could respond, they heard two loud and pronounced knocks on the apartment door. Derek held his arm out in a gesture to keep Siobhan back out of the way as he looked through the peephole. He turned back at Siobhan in confusion, and unlocked the door, opening it. Julia stood in front of them flanked by two very large and very thin-featured men. Behind her stood another woman of around her height with a stare that could cut steel.

"May we come in child?" Julia smiled kindly, putting her phone in the pocket of her wool blazer. Derek stepped back and allowed the group to pass.

"Julia. I'm sorry. We weren't expecting you to…" Siobhan said as she searched for something to pull her pillow-styled hair back. "How did you get into the building?"

"Not to worry child, we thought a face-to-face was necessary. And locks on doors are typically only deterrents," Julia grinned.

"The Order," she paused, giving a slight glance to the pale man on her right, "Feels the situation is a little dire than first thought. They also believe your assistance with the Succubae's apprehension is paramount."

Her voice was kind and soft, but a slight hint of disagreement could be felt in the air.

"Funny," Derek eyed the group with suspicion, "I actually was thinking the same thing but…I have some questions first."

The pale man to Julia's right grunted slightly with disapproval and Julia's eyes snapped back at him with a warning but her voice remained even, "I do feel introductions are in order first, my child. Then all questions will be answered."

Turning to face her companions, she smiled warily, "Derek and Siobhan, please let me introduce High Counselor Luther of the royal Ne` de Sang court," she moved her hand to indicate the man to her immediate right.

"This," using the same gesture to indicate the man to her left, "Is High Counselor Silas of the royal court of Montagne Blanche."

Julia then moved to one side, allowing the striking woman behind her to move forward, "And this is Captain Tara Vena of the High Elven Green court."

After Julia's introduction was complete, all three bowed slightly at Derek and Siobhan.

"Now, my child, to what questions do you seek answers? Please be quick because time is short, and we have a lot to discuss," Julia stated rather firmly.

Derek, continuing to eye the group with escalating suspicion, sniffed the air and wrinkled his nose as if he detected something unpleasant. He and Siobhan both took note of the pale men's expressions as he did this. Derek chose to ignore it for now and asked, "I know you're a witch, Julia, but what are they?"

Julia nodded, "Counselor Luther and Counselor Silas are of vampire origin, Captain Tara Vena is elf-kind."

At that moment, Captain Vena moved the hair from around her face to reveal ears that had profound points at the tip.

"All three are members of the Order's Forhelien Charge. Their purpose is much like the Known's military Special Forces or Navy Seals if you will," Julia explained.

"Wow. Isn't this a little heavy-handed, I mean, you said Succubae are dangerous but, isn't this..." Siobhan said hesitantly.

"Overkill," Derek finished for her flatly. "It seems like overkill. Why all the muscle?" He looked pointedly at Luther, to which Luther raised a dark eyebrow.

"Is there a reason you mistrust us so quickly?" Luther's baritone voice asked playfully.

Without hesitation, Derek said, "Yeah, you stink."

Low growls emanated from both Luther and Silas with the latter moving swiftly to drop a short spear from the arm of his black coat and point it at Derek's neck. Siobhan let out a muted yell while the elf Tara began to laugh heartily, "Yes brother, they do have their own special... *odor*."

It was Julia that brought control to the room again, "Enough!" she shouted.

At once all parties stood down and took a step back.

"For the love of the heavens, our goal is to apprehend this Succubus, not perpetuate a schoolyard squabble. You Forhelien should know better! You all know what's at stake," she hissed.

The tone in the room immediately shifted. The Forhelien were no longer sneering at each other or Derek and Siobhan; they were somber and refocused.

Julia's voice returned to its pleasantness, "Now, the Order has a plan to draw out the Succubus and her mate, but" she hesitated, "It would require your participation, my child."

"Von and I have already agreed to do something, whether you invited us or not. I won't sit by and wait for her to hunt *me*," Derek asserted.

Tara hissed an almost gleeful, "Yes." Her eyes smiled and shone like pale green crystals.

"Good," Julia said in agreement then turned to Siobhan, "And what of your answer child? You have spoken little."

Siobhan stood with quiet resolve for several seconds then turned and looked at Derek.

"Oh," she smiled confidently, "I'm all in."

"Excellent," Julia nodded curtly, turning to the Forhelien, "You will begin the preparations."

The trio all bowed respectfully at her, turned, and headed out the door, shutting it behind them. At this, Julia gave a heavy sigh and turned back to face Siobhan and Derek. "Dealing with adult children, no matter the kin... is exhausting. Please, let's sit," she made her way to the living room chair and sat slowly.

"Julia, are you alright?" Siobhan asked.

She sighed again, "Sweet child, dealing with the Order, especially those in the higher levels of the council, can wear on an old woman. But we have our own things to discuss."

She gestured for the pair to sit across from her, and they complied. "Now, we don't have much time, Luther and Silas will be back shortly to take you to a safer place...."

"Wait, what?" Derek interrupted.

Julia looked at him exasperated, "Please, child, let me speak. I need to tell you things before there are others around. The Order wishes that I not tell you the things I am about to... I disagreed. I feel as though you should see more of the...*bigger* picture. There are many things at play here, my child... many more things than you realize, and many I just can't explain right now. But let me tell you what I can."

She knew she had their full attention and she continued on, "Derek, there are things about your birth family that you will soon discover. I can't go into details now, but just know that when the time is right, I will explain everything. But who your family is may be the reason this succubus has sought you. She is very cunning which clearly makes her more dangerous... That's why it's imperative that you be part of her capture... you're the key. And don't let the Forhelien intimidate you... Luther and Silas are honorable and are good in a fight... you'll need them before this is over... Tara is loyal and will lead fiercely; trust her. Lastly, you must trust each other. You *will* be tested before this is over and you must not forget your bond."

She closed her eyes and nodded, "We're out of time. Please, grab what you can and go with them." Before she could hear arguments or questions from either of them, she rose and left the apartment.

A moment later, two hard, familiar knocks were heard. Siobhan quickly opened the door to see Luther and Silas standing shoulder to shoulder.

"We're here to escort you to an Order safe house," Luther said with an air of authority.

Siobhan craned her neck out of the window just in time to see Julia climb into the back of a dark sedan with tinted windows. Just as it sped away, Luther looked down his nose at Siobhan. She smiled back at him sweetly as she turned back into the room to start packing.

7

Twenty minutes later, Siobhan and Derek had packed a duffle bag each with only essentials and were speeding up the Five Highway in the back of another nondescript dark blue sedan. Silas and Luther occupied the front seats while Siobhan and Derek sat behind them, neither pair spoke for several minutes. Siobhan looked at the back of their heads and then at Derek apprehensively. Her uncertainty and uneasiness emanated from her so much that even Derek could feel it. Reaching out, he took her hand on the seat and squeezed gently. Her soft hand slightly trembled under his and he stroked her fingers gently in an effort to calm her.

Remembering Julia's advice, Derek cleared his throat loudly, "I need to know where you're taking us."

Silas, who was driving, glanced at him in the rearview mirror. "To a safe house," he replied dryly.

Derek rolled his eyes, "Look, don't be an asshole...you know what I'm getting at...where is this safe house?"

It was Luther that responded with a little more politeness as he looked over his shoulder, "North and near the riverfront. We should be arriving in about forty-five minutes."

Siobhan and Derek both took note of the eye roll and derisive snort from Silas. Derek glanced over at her, gave Siobhan a reassuring smile and he squeezed her hand as he continued to hold it. He wanted her to feel safe and to know that he would protect her. He just hoped he could convey all those thoughts without words.

The car continued to race up the highway at a smooth speed. No one spoke for the rest of the drive and Derek never released his hold on Siobhan's hand. The whole trip her eyes were wide, and she seldom blinked. She tried to control her own breathing, but it was short and shallow. In her mind, she begged Derek not to let go of her hand because she just felt so overwhelmed at the moment by the speed at which this situation was moving.

In the last twenty-four hours, they had learned that witches, vampires, and elves were real. Not just that, but her closest and best friend was a victim of a succubus, and from the vagueness of Julia's explanation, she may or may not have some other knowledge or connection to everything else in his life. Siobhan could feel her heart starting to beat faster, so she took several deeper breaths to clear her mind. She looked over at Derek and watched him; she could sense the tension he was holding also.

He sat stiffly in the seat next to her. He must be furious that Julia dropped ambiguous information in his lap and cut him off from asking questions. Derek didn't even know anything about his birth family, how could Julia? She watched his jaw muscles flex, and he kept his eyes bouncing between their vampire escorts and the road ahead. His eyes and the tender stroke of his fingers on hers were the only movements he made, but she could see the wheels in his head turning.

The car began to slow into an area of the city known for corporate office buildings and industrial manufacturing. The car crept a little more with every turn and before they knew it, Silas was pulling into a parking space in an otherwise empty lot. The older building before them was clearly empty but not unkempt. Derek made a mental note that it was indeed a safer location as it was nestled between and behind several other taller buildings. One would have to know what they were looking for to find it.

Several feet in front of the parking space were a heavy steel fire door; its dirty gray paint chipped at the edges. Silas swiftly moved from the driver seat of the sedan to the door and stood guard. With the same type of blinding movement, Luther had also exited the car, removed the bags from the trunk, and positioned himself back next to Siobhan's door.

Derek and Siobhan stared at each other in disbelief. He gave her hand one more soft squeeze and leaned into her car, "We'll be okay. It's you and me... no matter what, we stay together."

He searched her face for any flicker of doubt or fear, but he found none; what he did find was resolve.

She nodded sharply and whispered back, "Together."

Just inside the old gray door, a dimly lit hallway led to several empty offices on either side. Walking in a single file with Silas leading the way, Luther carried the bags behind them. Silas stopped abruptly and tilted his head, seemingly to listen to something unheard by either human companion. Derek glanced back at Luther to find him stone-faced and listening to the same unheard sounds.

"Hey... guys... want to clue us in?" Derek whispered hoarsely.

"Nothing. False alarm," Luther stated in a normal voice and moved forward.

Silas took a few more steps, reaching out to open another set of double doors. Derek and Siobhan could see warm light spilling into the hallway in front of them and watched Silas bow deeply toward the door. The pair were cautious as they rounded the corner and stepped into the glow of the biggest conference room either of them had ever seen. At its center, a large, long wooden table of golden-colored wood sat. Its edges were intricately carved with scrolls and leaves and the same pattern adorned the chairs surrounding it. On the table, at every seating space, was a file folder, a pen, and a glass. It looked as though they were interrupting a board of directors meeting for a medieval king.

It took the pair a moment to shift their eyes down to the far-left side of the table. Standing beautifully poised was Julia wearing long, heavy robes of dark green and purple. She looked like something out of a fairy tale with her softly greying hair cascading down her back with two braids that framed her face on either side. She wore a large silver crescent moon around her neck and her fingers were encircled with several versions of moon phases, all cast in silver. Her dark round eyes were softly focused on the group as they entered the space. She gestured with her hand for them to find a place around the table to sit.

Derek and Siobhan took the two seats just to the left of Julia while Luther and Silas sat across from the pair on her right. Just as they were sitting, a door behind Julia opened and Captain Vena strode inside flanked by another elf on her right and someone entirely different on her left. Neither Derek nor Siobhan knew what the *person* was to the captain's left, but they both guessed a member of the Fae. The trio filled in all but the two remaining seats with Captain Vena sitting directly to Derek's left.

Once Julia was satisfied all were in attendance, she smiled sweetly, "Thank you all for your promptness."

With her words, she sat slowly in her own seat, raising her inter-locked fingers to her lips, "I believe introductions are in order, Captain Vena."

"Yes, your Sovereign. Derek, Siobhan allow me to introduce you to Lieutenant Abhainn Abor of the Meadowlands Court," she directed their attention to the male on her left whom they recognized as elf-kind. "And this is Fae Zhaar."

Zhaar immediately rose from his seat, his shock of spiked white hair seemed to glow under the soft lights of the room. He bowed a deep reverent type of bow to Derek, his thin hands laying seemingly very delicate on his torso, "It is an honor to serve."

Julia cleared her throat loudly, "Thank you Zhaar and Lieutenant for coming on such short notice. If you all will open your files, you will see the surveillance photos that have been retrieved for us by our were-folk yesterday..."

Derek made to raise his hand, "Uhm, excuse me?"

"Yes, my child?" Julia asked patiently.

"Were-folk?"

Julia nodded, "Yes, we have set two of the Forhelien werewolf members out already. They excel in tracking and should report back here shortly."

She turned to Luther and Silas, "Transfer report?"

"We were not followed your Sovereign. Casius had eyes on both targets while the transfer took place and would have alerted us. We had no incidents." Luther's baritone voice confirmed, and Silas nodded his agreement.

"Excellent. We will wait for Casius or Alder to return with an update before moving. As you can see from the pictures in front of you, it is indeed the succubus Daria and her mate Alexis. And from our information provided by Derek and Siobhan," Julia nodded at them, "We can now confirm why she has come out of the shadows after so long. We must keep our focus at the forefront. Daria cannot be allowed to bring this Chirion to birth. Both worlds depend on this goal. Too long as she and her kin skimmed the edges of our worlds looking to wreak destruction and chaos. We are lucky we've found allies in our human friends and that they've agreed to assist us… without them this mission is folly."

"Exactly, what *is* our role here?" Derek asked. He was quickly growing tired of the strong feeling he had that they weren't getting the full picture. He had so many questions running through his mind and now wasn't sure he would get direct answers.

"I mean, look around this table. I see two vampires, elves, and a fae, and there are *werewolves* running around playing spy… all for what? Because there's a she-demon that poisoned me, then fucked me for my…" Derek's anger had begun to show but his words were cut off by Siobhan.

"DNA," Siobhan interrupted.

"Right. My DNA," Derek nodded his approval at her.

"What is your point, human?" Silas growled.

"My point?" Derek snorted, "My point is why? Why is this such a big deal to *any* of you? Especially, you…you seem to know a hell of a lot about me…" he pointed a finger directly at Julia.

A guttural low growl came from somewhere deep inside Silas and jumping from his seat, slammed his hands down on the table. His strength betrayed him as the table rocked heavily back and forth after he did.

"Insolence! How dare you speak to her Sovereign in that tone! If you were not something more than a bag of flesh, I would teach you a lesson you wouldn't forget," his voice thick with a distinct French accent as it thundered.

Siobhan jumped to her feet, standing between Derek and the rocking table. "You would have a fight like no other on your cold hands," she said, her tone matching Silas's.

Siobhan could feel Derek's tense body pushing into her as he yelled over her head, "I barely know any of you. And as you pointed out, I'm human, I don't follow the same rules as you. Right now, all she has given us is half-truths and hazy explanations."

Derek continued on pointedly at Julia, "What *exactly* are you the Sovereign of?"

Silas's growling was met by an even lower rumbling from Luther. But it was Julia who spoke the loudest, "Enough! All of you."

She looked down at her hands for a moment before she spoke again, this time a little more softly. "Sit down," she looked directly at Silas, "All of you."

Julia took a moment while they returned to their seats in piercing silence. She turned to face Derek and Siobhan and gave them a wary smile, "I admit I have only given you half-truths and I know I haven't been able to clarify a lot of information for you... most of which is for your own good." Derek opened his mouth and started to interrupt, but Julia cut him off.

"My position and title in the Hidden are well regarded, but for those in the Known, well..." she sighed heavily, "They wouldn't understand. You see when I speak of the Order, I'm speaking of myself and a select group of representatives in the Hidden. One elder member from each head family of every caste of beings in the Hidden makes up our council."

"A very long time ago, our world was divided. Then, members of the witch House of Silver Light began to ally themselves with others in the Hidden. Witches have always had a good relationship with Elves and the Fae, but our early days with the Vampire and Werewolf families were tumultuous. We came to a point where we would see our own destruction if we didn't make accords and agreements, so that's what we did. Our treaties have held strong for hundreds of years, and while there have been disagreements on occasion, we've built a fairly peaceful existence… the House of Silver Light plays its role in that peace."

"What kind of role is that?" Siobhan asked directly.

Julia nodded her head acquiescing, replying, "One of leadership. We, witches, have always tried to make peace where we can. In a different age, our ancestors were known as healers and magicians but most importantly, we were excellent mediators. These traits were well respected among all beings but have been forgotten by all except those around this table. It's why long ago, the Great Council created within the treaty, the Order, with a witch sitting at its head. More to your point though, the full title that is given to me is Her Sovereignty, Lady of Argentum Lucem… I am Julia of the House of Silver Light; I am the ruler of the Hidden."

Siobhan's eyes widened in surprise, and she looked over at Derek. He nodded his head and rolled his eyes as if he were given the information he already knew. Everyone around the table remained silent, except for Silas.

His dark eyes seemed to burn with hatred at Derek so much so that he couldn't stay quiet any longer, "She has protected you this entire time. You owe her more than respect. She is…"

A look that flew like a hundred knives radiated from Julia's face, "Silas! I said enough."

She turned back to Siobhan and Derek, "I'm sorry my child for hiding this from you. I never meant to lead you astray. Please, accept my apology." Her voice was soft and gentler than either of them expected.

Derek stared at Silas for a moment before he turned to Julia and spoke, "I don't like secrets… especially when it's my and Von's lives on the line. We agreed to help you, we didn't ask for your help… if I thought Daria would just go away on her own, we wouldn't be here now. I'll help you as long as we can agree that there are no more lies."

He turned back and continued staring down Silas' seething face.

Julia considered Derek for a moment then nodded, "Agreed child... no further lies."

She sighed heavily, then spoke to the entire table again, "We must be prepared to strike fast and hard. Tara, you, Luther, and Abhainn make certain Derek and Siobhan are prepared. Silas, you will find Casius... we'll need to move quickly, and we need whatever information they have."

With a nod of her head again, everyone except Derek and Siobhan rose from the table and began to busy themselves.

Tara moved closer to speak directly to the pair, "We will give you a moment to find your rooms and get settled. Please meet me back here in an hour for an assessment."

Before either could respond, Tara turned on her heel and left the room.

8

—⋅—

Derek and Siobhan found themselves down another small hallway lined with offices that had been converted into sleeping
quarters. Each room was identically decorated with an extra-long twin
bed sitting along the opposite wall from the door, and a small night-
stand with a brass lamp at the head. In a corner next to the door sat
a wooden table and a wheeled office chair. The rooms were painted a
neutral blue and there were no outside windows, but a fan hung down
from each ceiling to offer some movement of air. They chose the first
two rooms in the hallway next to each other.

Siobhan sat on the edge of the bed in deep contemplation when
Derek knocked on her door, "Hey, can I come in?"

"Yeah," she responded with a start.

"Sorry… didn't mean to scare you," he apologized as he made
his way to the black leather chair in the corner. Running his hands
through his hair, he leaned forward resting his arms heavily on his
knees. He was tired, he was angry, and he was drained.

"Nope. Just getting used to the surroundings," Siobhan said with a
half-smile.

She recognized the weariness on his face.

"Hey," she leaned in closer and patted his arm reassuringly, "We're
okay… We made it this far… we're closer now than we were last night."

He shook his head, "I'm sorry, Von... I never should have gotten you into this."

"As if you could have stopped me," she said defiantly.

"Still..."

"Look, like you said, we'll get to the bottom of this together... And I see that look on your face, you still think Julia is hiding something... I think you're right. She clearly hasn't been telling us the whole story and now she is holding on to information that is kinda important to you. Don't you remember when you first met? She said Daria came after you because of *who* you are, then her cryptic message in my apartment about your family? Well... who are you and what else does she know?" Siobhan mused.

Derek blinked at her in surprise; he hadn't really thought about that first conversation. All he had was a gut feeling that there were things that they were being kept in the dark about. His natural instinct about people had always been weirdly spot on. Even as a small child, he knew almost within minutes of meeting a new host family if they were good people or not. He thought again about his first conversation with Julia and considered Siobhan's question for a moment but the disappointment at no real insight crept back.

"Nobody... *really*. I'm a foster kid... I've never had parents or family. I've been on my own my whole life. There isn't anything that makes me special... I mean, nothing that should have drawn *that* kind of attention," he said.

Siobhan eyed him, "All I'm saying is that *she* slipped up. And if she has, someone else will too... it's a matter of time."

Derek's acceptance was encouraging, "We need to keep our ears open... you may be right, someone else may know something."

At that moment, two loud knocks rapped on the door. Startled, Derek and Siobhan stared at each other for a split second before Siobhan answered, "Who is it?"

From behind the heavy wooden door, they heard a familiar voice, "Captain Vena. Your presence is requested in the gym."

After a quick change into appropriate training attire as Captain Vena requested, Siobhan, Derek, and the elf made their way down a flight of stairs and through yet another set of heavy gray fire doors, and what lay beyond was the dream of every gym-rat enthusiast. The room was the size of four full-size basketball courts. At the far end of the room, opposite the doors, tumbling mats covered the floor and mirrors lined the entire wall. To the trio's immediate left was a full setup of weight machines, free weights, and cardio equipment. However, Captain Vena strode quickly across to the far right of the space where a large boxing ring stood. Siobhan and Derek just shrugged their shoulders at each other, following obediently.

Luther and Abhainn were already inside the ropes when they arrived, both men standing silently stoic and staring at each other. Abhainn nodded slightly at Luther and immediately both men brandished weapons and took defensive postures. Luther twirled the shiny, curved, machete-like knives with expert skill. He held one in each hand, and they danced and played in the air like ribbons. Abhainn reached behind his back and seemingly out of thin air a long wooden staff that was nearly as tall as the elf appeared.

Siobhan glanced over at Captain Vena, watching her eyes twinkling with delight as she called out, "Watch the underhand of the blade, Abhainn."

A wide creepy grin spread like oil over Luther's pale face. His teeth were large and white and his canine's deadly sharp. He kept his eyes focused on Abhainn but responded directly to Tara.

"Tsk tsk... Captain. It's not fair for your Lieutenant to have an extra set of eyes."

It was at that moment both men lunged for each other, and the battle began. Luther swirled the blades with elegant proficiency. Abhainn dodged and weaved his way around them as if he knew their movement. He lunged, flipping his staff quickly, and caught Luther in the side. The vampire gave a barely noticeable wince and advanced on the elf. Abhainn flipped his staff again and clipped the vampire under his chin. A small droplet of thick, deep red blood trickled slowly from the open wound. Luther slid back swiftly, touching his finger to his chin, wiping the heavy droplet from the cut. His eyes narrowed as he grinned salaciously at the elf.

Luther began to twirl the left blade in arcs as he came upon Abhainn with smooth, swift movements. Before Abhainn could react, the vampire slid with lightning speed around Abhainn, positioning himself behind the elf, grabbing him by the throat, and slamming him to the ground. Luther then wrapped the curved blades on either side of the elf's exposed throat like scissors. Both Siobhan and Derek thought the fight was finished, but Abhainn quickly rolled to his stomach while sliding across the ring as if it were covered in oil. With the same smooth movement, he got to his feet and shoved Luther forward knocking him off balance for a moment.

Luther spun and let out a low growl that was felt more than heard as he spun his blades in tight circles around him and again advanced upon the elf. The pair created a beautiful dance of advancements and retreats, each one laying blows upon the other in turn. The duo seemed like well-paired sparring partners and Siobhan was fascinated by how gracefully each of them moved and even more impressed by how each of them answered the other person's offense. It was a beautiful conversation in motion. It was again Luther's turn to advance on the elf. His right blade began making large arcs in the air when Abhainn made his mistake; an error that Siobhan could see would end this fight.

As Luther's blade swished through the air, Abhainn drew his staff forward in an attempt to block the knife and use the momentum to push through Luther. However, Abhainn missed the second blade as Luther made a shortcut under the arcing one and stopped the staff altogether. Using the knives, Luther flipped the staff out of the elf's hands, throwing Abhainn to the ground. The vampire seized the opportunity to kneel on the elf's chest, both blades at Abhainn's throat. The battle was won.

Both men were breathing hard as the gathered audience around the ring clapped. Luther stood from Abhainn's chest, offering his hand. The elf took it and rose to his feet. Both vampire and elf bowed to each other and exited the ring.

Derek and Siobhan heard Captain Vena whisper to Abhainn, "Told you about the blade."

Abhainn shrugged slightly, taking a bottle of water from her.

"Okay, now it's your turn," Captain Vena turned to Derek and Siobhan.

Siobhan raised an eyebrow, "Our turn for...what exactly?"

The captain stepped upon the ring and ducked under the ropes, "I don't care which one of you goes first but choose."

Siobhan and Derek stared at each other while having a silent conversation. Vena became impatient, "Fine... Derek in the ring with me."

Derek turned to Siobhan, "Not to be *that* guy, but...," he looked over his shoulder at Vena, "I don't hit women. You wanna take this one?"

Siobhan, her voice low, got so close to Derek, he could feel her warm breath on his cheek, "It won't matter... this isn't about being chivalrous. We aren't dealing with normal rules... just do what you have to."

Derek nodded in understanding. He pulled himself into the ring and whispered under his breath, "Wish me luck".

Vena nodded at Derek and from her waist bowed to him, "We will use no weapons. We are merely training. Please don't hold back."

Derek responded in kind, bowing at his waist to Vena. He got into a fighting stance and waited for Vena to advance first.

Captain Vena threw the first punch, making contact with the center of his chest. The blow threw Derek back and against the ropes. He didn't fall to the mat, but the look of surprise on his face couldn't be missed. Siobhan watched Luther and Silas snicker. It was then that Siobhan realized that there were two more distinctively different men standing ringside.

They were both taller than average height, she estimated around six foot eight. But they both had two features that were even more outstanding: first, both men looked like they were the apex of health; muscles wide and rippling even under their silk, button-up shirts. She wondered to herself how they were even able to get them on.

Second, the duo had thick heads of hair that hung to the middle of their backs and looked both stylish and oddly unkempt simultaneously. She thought they were both classically handsome but there was also something off about the pair. Their eyes were just a little too big and the nostrils a little too large. Like a light had been turned on in her head, it came to her: these were canine features.

'*Werewolves,*' she thought. The men she was staring at had to be Casius and Alder.

She turned her attention back to the ring in time to see Derek throw an almost perfectly executed roundhouse that caught Vena at the base of her neck. Vena flew forward but jumped unnaturally high in the air, turned, and landed back on her feet in front of Derek.

"You know," Derek's breath labored, "You having special abilities isn't really a fair fight for a mere human like me."

Vena smiled back and breathed just as heavily, "C'mon brother, dig deeper. You have more tools deep inside you... Use them."

With her final words, she spun and landed a backhanded fist on the side of Derek's head. The blow threw him to the ropes, and he grabbed onto them for balance. Derek faced Vena again and they cycled through punches and blocks. The movements became faster and more precise as they fought. Siobhan watched in wonder as it looked like Derek was learning to anticipate his opponent's moves; she was impressed. Derek and Captain Vena danced around the ring for several minutes, neither one overcoming the other.

Taunting him, Vena asked, "Are you tired, human? Should we rest?"

That was the push Derek seemed to need to finish the bout. He moved quickly to his left to avoid a throw to his head. He simultaneously grabbed Vena's wrist and spun her away from him and shoved her forward. She recovered quickly, turning back to face him. As she did, he was ready for her. Drawing from some power within, Derek delivered an open-handed blow to the center of her chest that sent her reeling. She fell to the floor of the ring, landing on her back.

The entire gym was quiet as everyone watched the interaction unfold. Siobhan glanced over at Luther and Silas, who were no longer laughing, but on their feet seemingly ready to defend their sister-in-arms. Vena lay still for a moment as Derek stood directly over her. He reached out his hand for the assist. Vena took it smiling as he helped her to her feet and the pair bowed to each other.

Vena glanced over at Siobhan and grinned, "Can your friend fight as well as you?"

"Why don't you ask *her*?" Rolling sweat fell off Derek's temples as he chuckled.

"Maybe I will," Vena laughed openly as she made her way to the side where Siobhan stood. "You next?"

Siobhan, still keeping an eye on Luther and Silas, responded with a curt, "Yep," as she entered the ring.

She turned pointedly to Vena and said, "But, not with you."

Vena looked almost hurt at her words, "Certainly... who do you choose as a partner then?"

Without taking her eyes off Vena, Siobhan pointed at Silas, "Him."

"Are you sure?" She whispered, cutting her eyes in Silas's direction. "Maybe Abhainn or I would be better suited for our first training... not a Vamp..."

Siobhan cut her off, turning in Silas's direction, "I'm sure. You ready smart ass?"

A look of shock and oily delight came over Silas's face. Derek moved between Siobhan and Silas.

"What are you doing?!" he said in a frantic and hoarse whisper. "You can't take him. Von! Listen to me."

She stared up at Derek and smiled, "Trust me... please."

"I do trust *you*," he hissed between clenched teeth. "Please don't do this... please Von."

His dark eyes read anger and fear as they pleaded with her. Siobhan reached up and cupped his face in her hands, drawing it close to hers. Derek found their warmth comforting.

She leaned in and said softly, "I've always got your back. Always."

She leaned back and nodded slightly at him, and he begrudgingly left the ring. Silas entered the ring with a swift jump over the top rope. Arching his back, he stretched his arms and worked the tension out of his joints.

His lips spread wide in an evil grin across his pallid face, "Are you certain you want to enter a fight with me, *human*?"

Siobhan stared deadly into Silas's cold eyes, "You've got a big mouth, Vampire."

Vena's voice rang clear from the side of the ring, "This is just *training* Silas... A training."

She emphasized the word again as a warning.

Silas only smiled as he took position and bowed. Siobhan bowed back, took her stance, and waited for Silas to strike. As she predicted, the vampire rushed her, throwing a front punch to her face. Siobhan sidestepped quickly and Silas missed by feet. Without turning to face him, Siobhan ducked to miss the second blow Silas attempted to the back of her head. With a smooth movement, she threw her own front punch but hers made contact with the vampire's nose. It made a soft *crack* upon impact and dark red, nearly black, blood trickled slowly out of both nostrils. Silas's face was one of shock and anger as he wiped the blood away with his hand.

The vampire advanced on her again and they locked each other in a blurring sequence of punches, jabs, kicks, and blocks as they continuously moved forward on each other. Siobhan was finally able to get the vampire's arms in a lock and she threw him to the ground. But as she did, he was able to get a hand around one of her ankles and she tumbled to the mat. They both pulled themselves to their feet concurrently, but the vampire was a little quicker and grabbed Siobhan by the arm and threw her violently into the turnbuckle. Another soft crack was heard as her rib cage made contact.

Siobhan realized she had stayed on her knees for a moment too long as Silas's leg made contact with the other side of her rib cage. She heard Derek's loud protest to Vena to end the fight. But Siobhan knew she had Silas where she wanted him and shook her head emphatically. She had walked into the ring to teach Silas a lesson and that is what she intended to do. She wanted him arrogant with the thought he bested the human.

As the vampire came in for a second kick to her ribs, Siobhan reached over and grabbed his planted foot, dropping the vampire to the ground. She immediately made hard and quick contact with his solar plexus with her elbow. She threw herself on his chest, pinning his arms to the ground with her knees, and finished him with two sharp punches to the center of his face with her fist. She jumped up, backing away quickly before the vampire could react.

Blood rolled from Silas' upper lip and nose now. He swiftly stood as the group around them clapped, indicating to him the match was done. He bowed to Siobhan and without conceding to her victory said flatly, "You might still make a worthy opponent."

Siobhan's expression remained flat as she bowed back.

Vena met Siobhan as she exited the ring, "Well done sister! I don't think Silas has been beaten like that in quite some time."

"I told him he had a big mouth," Siobhan said with a wry smile. Derek held the ropes for her as she leaned out of them and eased herself out of the ring. Her sides hurt but they wouldn't kill her; she'd live.

"Are you in need of medical assistance?" Abhainn asked.

She shook her head, "Nah, I've been worse...I've got it."

"I think that's enough for today...we've got time to get you both in shape before we face Daria," Vena smiled.

With that Vena and Abhainn nodded their approval and turned to leave the gym. Derek and Siobhan stood facing each other alone in the large space. His eyes looked over her as if checking for other signs of distress.

"Damn," he stated.

Siobhan's face flushed quickly.

"What?" she smiled coyly.

Derek offered his arm for assistance, and she took it graciously. They walked arm in arm halfway across the gym before he spoke, "Well...I realized how lucky I am."

She shot him a look of bewilderment, laughing, "How lucky *you* are?"

"Yeah, I'll never insult your driving... ever again. I don't want to end up like that."

He threw a thumb in the direction of the ring and laughed loudly. Siobhan only rolled her eyes and joined in his merriment.

Derek helped her back to their rooms and brought her wrap to stabilize her cracked ribs. Siobhan found a couple of ibuprofens in the bottom of her bag and took them to stave off the pain. This certainly was not the worst she had ever been hurt and the satisfaction it brought her knowing that she diminished at least a little of Silas's smugness made it all worth it.

Soon after, a woman who identified herself as Julia's handmaiden, Asha, brought trays of food and drinks to Derek and Siobhan's respective rooms. They thanked her for the food and asked if they could speak to Julia. The handmaiden explained that her Sovereign had already retired for the evening, but she would relay the message to Julia in the morning. With a quick turn, she left the room.

"Maybe this is better... we both need to get some rest and god knows what's in store tomorrow," Siobhan said with a heavy sigh.

"Yeah, you're right. It's late, we should probably turn in," Derek's voice trailed off as he realized how close he was standing to her. His heart and mind began to race furiously as he felt the heat from her body next to him. He realized he had been staring at her for too long and she was staring back.

Before he turned to leave, he leaned closer, kissing her softly on the cheek, "I'll see you in the morning."

Her green eyes smiled back at him, "Goodnight."

Derek shut the door as he left. He found his room and bed in pitch darkness and collapsed on it. He fought hard to push back the thoughts of Siobhan. They had seemingly come from nowhere and he knew there was no time to examine them right now as there was too much happening around them. He was ready for this nightmare to be over. He lay in the quiet, listening.

From where they were located, he couldn't hear even the faintest conversation. There were no whispers, no creaks of doors, no ambient noise whatsoever. The only sound was the gentle humming of his overhead fan.

'*Do the vampires sleep at night? Or even at all?*' he thought to himself. '*What about werewolves?*'

The questions poured over his mind until exhaustion overtook him.

9

— · —

A loud crash startled him awake. Jumping out of bed, Derek was on full alert as he ran to stand at his door. He didn't turn on the light so whatever was on the other side didn't have any indication he was ready for them. After a moment of stillness, he cracked the door open slightly, looking out but only a dim light showed around the corner of the hallway. Opening the door wider, he took a step out. He reached over to check Siobhan's door, but it was locked. Derek continued to move silently down the hallway toward the light. As he reached the corner, he peeked around to see the source of the illumination and as he did, he saw Silas and a very pale and very wide-eyed Siobhan.

Silas held her against the wall and slightly aloft with his right hand while his left hand forced her head back and toward Derek, her neck fully exposed. Her pupils looked fully dilated and fixed, and blood dripped from her gaping mouth. As Derek came fully around the corner Silas stopped, turning his head toward Derek. Thick blood trickled off his mouth as he licked his lips.

The same oily smile from earlier in the day spread across the vampire's face as he said, "I was looking for a midnight snack, and she is *so* delicious."

Heat seemed to rise in Derek's entire body as fury raced through him. With a primal roar, he charged the vampire and tackled him. Siobhan's limp body slid down the wall and to the floor as the two men wrestled in the dimness of the hallway. Derek got several hard blows to Silas's head quickly, but the vampire had unnatural speed and made quick work of freeing himself of the human.

"You son of a bitch! I will kill you!" Derek screamed as he continued to thunder toward the vampire.

Silas, spreading his arms open in a challenge, laughed at him, "Really? I will lay you out beside her if you like."

The fury fueled Derek as he leaped up, moving toward Silas again. The pair traded blow after blow with Silas being much faster than Derek and able to move with unnerving agility. But Derek never relented and continued to push harder, determined to kill the vampire. He landed a final roundhouse to Silas's head but again, Silas being much faster at the recovery, grabbed Derek's ankle before his foot touched the ground and with a loud *SNAP* broke it. Derek collapsed in excruciating pain and began backing away quickly from the vampire that towered over him now. He only stopped when he felt the coolness of Siobhan's arm on his.

"Do it already!" Derek growled with clenched teeth.

Silas stood over him baring his stone-white teeth then looked from Siobhan's corpse back to the bloodied man.

"No..." he whispered, "This is much more satisfying."

Silas smiled to himself, turned, and disappeared into the darkness.

Derek breathed heavily, sliding next to Siobhan. He pulled her lifeless body off the concrete floor toward him, laying her head in his arms. He brushed her auburn hair away from her face and stroked it gently. Tears streamed uncontrollably from his eyes and the fury he felt just moments ago was replaced by anguishing sorrow.

"No... no... no!" he wailed as he rocked her limp body in his arms. He reached down and pulled her eyelids closed over what used to be sparkling green eyes. The tears fell faster as he held her tight against his body.

10

—·—

"**N**o!" Derek heard himself yell as he sat up in bed.

Cold sweat poured down his face and mixed with the tears that streamed from his eyes. He surveyed his surroundings, listening closely but nothing moved as the room remained dark and quiet. After a moment of grasping back onto reality, he jumped out of bed, making his way into the hallway. Still, nothing moved, and the hallway was also dark. He could feel the edge of Siobhan's door and found her doorknob was locked. He took a deep breath and held it as he knocked softly. After what seemed like several minutes, he heard the soft *click* of the lock opening.

Dim light landed on the hall floor as a sleepy-eyed Siobhan looked out, "Reek? It's like three am...everything okay?"

Derek gave a long sigh and opened the door a little wider to take a look inside. Siobhan was dressed in an oversize tee shirt, cut-off sweatpants, and socks. Her long hair was gathered in a messy bun on top of her head, as she rubbed her eyes awake. Derek grabbed onto her fiercely, holding her tightly against him. She could feel every muscle in his body flex and tighten.

After a moment, she wrapped her arms around his waist and in a muffled voice said, "What's up? You, okay?"

Derek held her there a second longer before releasing a little, chuckling, "Um, yeah. I thought I heard something and needed to check on you."

She looked up at him and said, "I'm fine… Remember? I kicked a vampire's ass yesterday?"

As her eyes focused more, she could see his tear and sweat-stained face, "You're not okay… Jesus, what's wrong?"

Derek shook off her question and released her, "Nothing, I'm okay. Just you know, bad dream, heard a noise…I'm good now."

He looked at her for a long moment and shoved his hands deep into the pockets of his pajama pants.

"I'm gonna go back to bed… I'm sorry I woke you," he smiled. One quick kiss on her forehead and he made to leave the room.

"Hey," she grabbed onto his hand, "You sure you're alright?"

He played with her fingers in his and again, he recognized their warmth. He gave her a slight nod and said, "I'm good," and dropped her hand.

Siobhan stood in bewilderment until she heard the lock on his door latch. She shook her head and crawled back into her abandoned covers.

Daybreak quickly found them, and Derek waited for Siobhan to dress before the pair headed into the common area looking for breakfast. His head was pounding, and he knew his primary goal at that moment was caffeine. As they entered the conference room, the smell of salty bacon and rich coffee played with their senses. At the far right of the room, a long table was set up buffet-style with every sort of breakfast concoction they could want. They filled a couple of plates, grabbed some coffee, and headed toward the ornate conference table.

Sitting at the head of the table again was Julia while Captain Vena sat just to her right-hand side. Just a couple of seats down from her sat the two men Siobhan identified as Casius and Alder the previous day.

Julia motioned for Derek and Siobhan to sit next to her.

"Good morning my child! Did you sleep wel..." her voice trailed off as she stared into Derek's worn face.

"Gracious..." she lowered her voice to barely above audible, "I wonder if you slept at all."

"I managed," he said flatly.

Siobhan gave Derek a side glance and spoke to Julia, "Just an adjustment with everything. High anxiety situation...people trying to kill you... that sort of thing."

"Of course," Julia eyed Derek suspiciously, took a sip of her coffee, and addressed Siobhan again. "I was just speaking with Captain Vena about the activity in the training commons yesterday. She was extremely impressed with not only Derek but your performance as well."

Siobhan took a bite of toast, nodding, "I appreciate that. Although, I didn't find my sparring partner extremely impressed or *impressive*."

Derek and Vena both chuckled at this, but the Captain drew a sharp glance from Julia.

The darker headed of the two men at the table cleared his throat to speak, "Your Sovereign, don't look too harshly on the Captain...it was rather quite amusing to see Silas and his arrogance being tested."

Julia's face still showed a hint of disapproval, but she nodded slightly, "Still not an appropriate topic for breakfast conversation, Casius."

The werewolf shrugged.

Captain Vena rose from her seat, "Sovereign, I'll go prepare for the briefing."

Julia nodded as Vena continued speaking to the rest of the group, "We'll all meet back here in one hour, with the Brethren, for the daily briefing...it's possible we converge on the Succubus tomorrow."

She turned on her heel and strode off, carrying her plate and utensils with her. Derek and Siobhan stared in surprise after her and at each other.

"Who are the Brethren?" asked Siobhan.

"Our infantry soldiers. Everyone here has served in the Brethren," the lighter-headed man explained.

Siobhan nodded in understanding, "All Forhelien are Brethren, but not all Brethren are Forhelien."

Alder grinned widely in amusement, "Yes. Forhelien has received specialized and elite training."

"We're making our move tomorrow?" Derek asked Julia.

Julia nodded solemnly. "Yes, my child. We need to move quickly. Casius and Alder," she nodded in the direction of the huge men who still sat at the middle of the table, "Have reported that Daria and Alexis are relocating their operations. Which means she has been impregnated and is carrying a Chiron. They'll want to isolate themselves for protection. We'll have to go forward with the plan now before they can complete their relocation...there'll be more training today and the Forhelien will equip you with weaponry. We'll need to move quickly when we strike."

She then smiled coyly at Siobhan, "I'm sure you will find Silas a little more palatable today."

Julia rose from her seat and motioned for the two werewolves to keep theirs as they nodded respectfully.

Derek and Siobhan sat in awkward silence for what seemed like hours, picking at the remnants of food on their plates. Alder's deep, gravelly voice broke the silence like a bubble, "We haven't been formally introduced... I am Alder Grey, and this is my brother, Casius."

Derek nodded to both in recognition and continued with his own introductions, "Derek Argent...and this is my friend Siobhan Miles... I guess I'm the one that caused this mess."

"Make no mistake friend, Daria is the cause," Casius replied. "She's been trouble from the beginning, more so than most Succubae... but the entire race...well...sucks."

His brother's comment made Alder chuckle, "Agreed. But she's crazier than most. She's got a real issue with the Great Treaty and she's power-hungry...she's the trifecta of nasty."

"Really?" Derek's interest was piqued.

"Hell yes," Alder maintained. "She's been a pain in the ass since Casius and I were cubs, and I'll be ninety-two soon."

"Holy shit. Seriously?" Siobhan blurted loudly, nearly choking on her coffee.

She stared at the brothers in wonderment. Both men *looked* to only be in their mid-thirties. Both were wide with broad shoulders that chiseled down to the fit physique of professional weightlifters. Siobhan couldn't even make out a facial wrinkle. It was difficult to believe they were old enough to be her grandparents.

Alder laughed heartily, his timbre low and bass, "Most factually... little brother Casius here will be eighty-eight...and we're still very much youngsters to our elders."

"So," Siobhan mused, "How old is Julia?"

Alder laughed again, "Witches are different...She's not as old as you might think."

"How so?" asked Derek.

"Witches are human. They will age as normal humans do. But they're magical and the stronger the witch, the more efficient they are at postponing the inevitable," Casius explained.

"How?" Siobhan pressed. This was the first time either of them felt like they were getting any direct answers. She was going to see how much she could get out of the pair.

Alder shrugged his wide shoulders, "Some create spells like glamours to stay young. I've heard others brew a special potion that slows aging...either will make a witch almost immortal."

"So, is everyone in the Hidden immortal?" Derek asked quizzically.

"Actually," Casius corrected, "We aren't really immortal. Although, to the human race we definitely look like it. We just age differently and live much, much longer... but we can be killed. Everything *can* die."

"Including a Succubus?" Derek asked.

"Including a Succubus," Casius assured firmly.

"Once we get close enough, that is," Alder corrected. "We can't miss...nothing worse than an impregnated succubae that's pissed off."

Siobhan, who was quietly absorbing the entire conversation, finally spoke again, "What do you mean, get close enough?"

"Succubae are quick and have the ability to dodge most projectiles long-range...great instincts. And the Incubae have an innate drive to protect their mates at *all* costs... if we aren't fast enough, Alexis will sacrifice himself for Daria, not a question about it, giving her a chance of escape," Alder said. "We have to be in remarkably close proximity and take them out simultaneously. We can't give them a moment to react."

"Julia seems to be taking this situation personally," Siobhan mused out loud.

The werewolf brothers made quick glances at each other before Alder spoke again softly, "She and Daria have a history. They first met when Julia was seventeen. It was well known that Julia's mother, Rosalind, would be stepping down as Sovereign when Julia turned twenty-one. The one thing Daria wanted more than anything is power."

"Still does," Casius added.

Alder continued, "Long story short, Daria conned her way up the royal ladder and tried to take everything away from Julia...including the love of her own mother."

"How so?" asked Derek.

"Subversion and lies. Daria did everything she could to ruin Julia's reputation in the court. It ran the gamut from poorly misplaced spells to murder...nothing was or *is* off-limits to Daria," explained Alder.

Siobhan stared incredulously, "Wait. You mean, Daria *killed* someone just to make Julia look bad?"

Alder nodded with emphasis, "Absolutely. Believe me, it wasn't the first time she had killed someone that stood in her way or the first person she destroyed to make a point. She's pure evil, even for a succubus...and it's all about power.

"I know this is a gruesome question," Siobhan continued delicately, "But exactly *how* do we kill a succubus?"

Casius looked at Alder then back at Siobhan, "Blessed projectile to the head. Bullet or arrow, it makes no difference."

He then smiled broadly at Siobhan, "Do you want to know how to kill a Vampire next?"

Casius and Alder roared with heavy laughter as Siobhan almost did another spit take. She was also laughing out loud before taking a quick glance at Derek. She sensed the bonding taking place in their small group, but she knew the slight look of consolation on Derek's face. He really wanted to know the answer to that question as well.

11

— · —

T he office in which Daria sat was decorated with expensive dark wood and leather furniture. She sat motionless at the large, presidential-style desk as the young woman standing beside her carefully placed the butterfly needle in the back of her hand. A small vacutainer slowly filled with the thin clear liquid. Daria breathed slowly and deliberately; her icy eyes focused on the younger woman.

The young woman was small in features with glowing red hair and the same icy blue eyes that Daria carried. Daria's stare made the younger woman nervous, and she shuffled a bit as she stood holding the needle steady. She decided it was better to concentrate on the task at hand than on the wide, hungry eyes of her boss.

The small test tube was nearly full when the young redhead laid her gloved hand over the small needle, pulling it from Daria's hand. The tiny wound left behind by the needle healed instantly as Daria blinked and smiled wryly at her assistant, "You know what to do with that, pet. And tell Alexis he can come in when you leave."

The small woman nodded, turned on her heel, and shut the heavy door behind her.

A few moments later, the chiseled face of Alexis sauntered through, "Darling, I'm not sure why you insist I wait outside while the little one is milking you."

He leaned down, kissing Daria on the cheek.

"Because" her malevolent smile wide, "I can't have you in here causing me a distraction while I work...thoughts of you could disturb my plans. Now...tell me about the mutt you saw."

Alexis sat on the desk in front of her, his eyes becoming suddenly worrisome, "We need to move soon sweet... I can't be sure, but I believe I saw Casius nearby, which means Alder isn't far behind. We can't risk our child's life by staying here."

Daria's eyes seemed to flare electric blue, and she stood, shoving the large leather chair against the wall behind her, "That bitch! She's called in her mercenaries!? Well, of course, she has... why would the delicate Queen of the Hidden come out from her castle door and fight me face to face when you can have the precious and mighty Forhelien at your beck and call?"

Daria stopped suddenly and mused for a moment at a bird tapping on the window in front of her. It couldn't see the succubus standing just inches from its tiny, frail body as it continued to *tap, tap, tap* at its own reflection. Daria began laughing wildly as the bird made a large loop and charged fully at the glass, giving its own life in the battle with itself.

Alexis stared after her, unphased by her outburst but waiting for the right moment to speak, "Daria, my love...?"

Still laughing, she faced him, "She hasn't told him."

"What?"

She licked her lips and the deviant smile returned to her face. Daria stood between Alexis's legs and kissed him.

"She. Hasn't. Told. Him," she emphasized every word carefully.

"I wonder what prophets wear? I feel like I should spread the good news," she cackled.

Alexis's understanding was clear, and his own slick smile spread.

"Daria, my sweet. Do you think that is a good idea? Think about this. Why lay all our cards out right now? No love... we should keep it close to us and they will never see it coming," he purred in her ear.

"But" Daria stuck her lip out in a child-like pout, "Why won't you let me have any fun?"

He pulled her closer and brushed his hand across her face. Wrapping both hands around the sides of her neck, he tilted her mouth to his. Lightly running his tongue over her lips, he kissed her softly, "You can have all the fun you want when you are sitting as Sovereign of the Hidden."

Daria giggled with delight.

12

—·—

The four had found the Sovereign's ladies-in-waiting waiting not very patiently for them to finish with their breakfast items so they could complete the morning clean-up. Once everything was handed over, they all headed toward the training room for weapons instruction. Derek's head still pounded like a marching band as they entered the brightly lit room. He squinted his disapproval at the fluorescent lights as they made their way across the expanse of the room.

Siobhan looked back at him concerned, "Hey...you, okay?"

"Yeah, just a headache," Derek shrugged.

Captain Vena stood in the middle of the ring again, waiting patiently for everyone to gather around the ropes. In her hand, she held a large carved staff made of light, glossy wood that was much like the staff Abhainn used the day before. At her feet lay a variety of swords, knives, and a bow. Derek took notice that there was not a gun in sight.

"Good morning," Vena stated strongly. "Today we will review our weapons training and allow our guests to become familiar with the different types we in the Brethren and Forhelien use most. Please break off in pairs and begin."

The group that stood around the perimeter of the ring dispersed throughout the gym and began setting up mock battles. Derek and Siobhan looked at each other with hesitation.

Vena noticed their seeming look of confusion and exited the ring, "No worries, you two are working with Alder, Casius, and myself...over here."

They followed Vena over to a table where the werewolf brothers displayed other various weaponry.

"Anything catch your fancy?" Casius asked.

"I've had some weapons training... I think I can get along with most of this," Siobhan responded as she picked up a curved blade with a thick handle made of dark marble.

Casius laughed heartily, "I'm certain you could! Still want to know which one kills a vampire efficiently?"

Siobhan and Casius glanced across to the far side of the room just as Silas lifted his head and glared back at them. Through his laughter, Casius spoke softer, "I'm only kidding Silas."

Siobhan watched Silas roll his eyes.

"He can hear you?" Siobhan asked incredulously. Alder pointed over in the vampire's direction as Silas nodded in the affirmative.

The friendly banter was interrupted by Derek, "So, this is going to kill a Succubus? What about a gun?"

Soft movements and clicks were heard throughout the gym.

"You mean like this one?" Vena asked as she pulled a small Glock 43 from her back.

Derek and Siobhan glanced around the room to find all the Brethren and Forehelien, including Luther and Silas, holding some fashion of handgun.

"We're of both worlds and we fight in both... just like you Derek," Vena said.

After a couple of hours of familiarizing themselves with the weaponry of the Hidden and having the opportunity to use the gun range attached to the gym complex, Derek and Siobhan made their way back to their respective rooms. Derek's headache had subsided quite a bit, but now hunger had overtaken him again. They found their rooms had been restocked with food and water and it came as a relief to Derek that he didn't have to spend any more time with Silas at that moment. After his nightmare the night before, he really hated that guy.

He just needed a moment to think. He knew Julia was still not telling him everything, but he couldn't put his finger on what it could be.

'What am I missing?' he thought to himself.

Maybe she knows Silas can't be trusted because he certainly didn't trust him. That dream seemed so real. And not just real but...really *real* as he was still in shock hours later that Siobhan was alive. As his food settled in and his brain worked in overdrive, Derek lay back on the pillows on his bed to think. It was all right in front of him if he could just put it all together.

Tap, Tap, Tap

The tapping became clearer and louder. Sitting up in bed, Derek looked at his phone; three o'clock. He didn't usually nap, but the past week at taken its toll on him. Another knock.

"Yeah... coming," he called out.

Making his way across the room, he opened the door. The hand-maiden stood resolutely on the other side and held a note in her hand. Reaching out to give it to him she said softly, "Sir. A message from our Sovereign Julia of Silver Light."

Derek took the note from her hand and motioned for her to come inside. He unrolled the parchment and began reading as confusion permeated his features. "What is she talking about? That she has as-signed you to me?"

The young woman bowed her head to Derek and shut the door behind her, "Her Sovereign feels that you need extra protection by your side. I have been trained alongside the Forehelien and can offer you an extension of the safeguards that you have now."

Derek noticed he towered over her. He stood about a foot and a half over Siobhan, but this woman was much smaller. Her hair looked dark under the traditional veil that was pinned to her head and her eyes sparkled like an ocean.

He smiled at her, "Yeah, I'm not sure *you* are what I need. Besides, have you seen my friend fight? She's pretty good."

The tiny woman moved closer to him. Her light gossamer dress made it look as though she glided across the floor.

She looked up at him, "I can also provide you with a companion detail. Something your friend can't or won't do."

Her fingers moved flirtatiously along the buttons of his shirt until her hands came to rest on his hips.

"Uhmm...yeah, see, last time I got involved with someone from your world she drugged and assaulted me... I'm gonna pass," Derek said sternly.

"I meant no harm, sir. I've been instructed to be a vehicle for your healing... I'm sorry to have failed you," the handmaiden began to cry softly.

"Oh. Shit...no. It's okay...I didn't mean to..." he guided her over to the bed and instructed her to sit.

Reaching over her, he grabbed a tissue from the table and handed it to the woman. He sat next to her and felt terrible for being so abrasive. What the hell was Julia thinking about sending this girl to him?

"Thank you, sir, you're very kind," the maiden said softly.

"I don't understand why Julia would think that I needed a *compan-ion*. That's the last thing I need right now," he said more to himself than to the handmaiden.

Without a word, the young woman stood and placed herself be-tween Derek's legs. She reached around her own back and opened the small, gold clasp at her neck. Her soft dress fell to the floor and other than her veil, she stood completely naked in front of him. Leaning in, she kissed him gently on the lips. They tasted of sweet strawberries, and he thought for a split second that maybe he did want a companion. He looked into her clear blue eyes and considered her for a moment.

"No... I'm not doing this," Derek's voice was firm as he swallowed hard, lowering his eyes to shield them from her inviting body.

"You'll be sorry...very sorry."

Derek raised his eyes but instead of finding the woman crying and naked she was fully dressed and filled with fury.

"Excuse me?" he asked.

She pointed a small dagger at his throat, "I said you'll be sorry."

A dark smile crept over her once kind face, "She's going to die... I will make sure of it. I will slit your little whore's throat and you will watch as the life seeps from her into the ground."

"I'm not sure what is going on, but I'm pretty sure you aren't a handmaiden," Derek said, hands raised.

"So easy to manipulate. So easy," the dark smile only grew larger as the maiden spoke. "I'll make sure you remember me," she made a small flick with her wrist and the dagger made contact with Derek's neck.

13

— · —

"Hey!" Derek jerked out of the bed, nearly falling to the floor. He reached up, touching his neck where the blade made contact, and felt a small trickle of blood. He breathed heavily, looking around the empty room. There was no handmaiden, no note, and the room was completely silent. He sat for what seemed like several minutes playing the previous scenario in his head. Was it all in his head? Was it a dream? Again, it felt like the fight with Silas. Real... but not. Derek thought he might be going crazy and considered insanity as a real possibility. But... there was blood on his neck; that part *was* real, and he just couldn't explain it away. As all the thoughts tumbled in his head there was a soft knock at the door. Derek sat frozen for several seconds until he heard a familiar voice on the other side.

"Reek. It's me...can I come in?" Siobhan's muffled voice said.

Derek opened the door quickly, looking over Siobhan's head down the hallway.

"What are you doing?" She looked up at him curiously.

"Nothing. Just looking," his voice trailed off.

"Uhm... okay.... hey, what'd you do to your neck?" Siobhan asked with light concern.

He touched the spot where the handmaiden's blade had nicked him and deflected the question, "Oh. Nothing. Shaving or something."

Suddenly, an excruciating pain radiated up Derek's spine and into his head.

"Oh, God! Uhh!" he screamed in agony.

"Derek!" Siobhan yelled as he practically collapsed on her, "What's wrong?"

"My head! Oh my God...make it fucking stop!" Derek yelled hoarsely.

Siobhan wrapped both arms around his waist as he leaned hard on her. She guided him to the bed and made him sit down. His head was pounding harder than it ever had and he didn't know if he could take much more of the crushing pain.

Siobhan rushed out quickly, returning with a couple of painkillers and a glass of water from her room.

"Here... take these," she demanded, shoving the pills and the glass in his hand.

His hands shook violently as he grasped onto the glass and downed the medicine. He laid back against the pillows and closed his eyes.

"Thank you," he mouthed.

Siobhan scanned the room and saw nothing out of place. An empty food tray sat on the desk and two empty water bottles lay in the trash can. Nothing indicated that anything was out of place or that anyone had been in his room. His headache was getting worse, and she knew if she couldn't figure out what was going on with him, Derek wouldn't be fit to face Daria.

Daria. DARIA.

As if a spark went off under her, Siobhan shot off the bed, ran to the conference room, and retrieved a cup of hot water. She moved as quickly as she could back to her room and opened the black velvet pouch Julia had given them days before. Dumping the remaining contents from the pouch into the mug, she stirred it with a spoon from her food tray. Racing back to Derek's room she pulled him by his wrist into a sitting position. He groaned as she shoved the hot mug into his hands.

"Drink," she demanded.

He groaned again.

"Goddamn, it Derek! Drink it!" she said so forcefully she was nearly yelling again.

Derek's eyes opened just enough to find the steaming liquid and guide his lips to it. He sipped slowly until it was just cool enough to take larger pulls. When he finished, he weakly handed the mug back to Siobhan, fell back, and closed his eyes to sleep.

Siobhan placed a pillow under his head and stood over him listening to him breathe until she was satisfied that he was comfortable. He looked peaceful, but she couldn't be sure; so, she waited. As she did, anger boiled inside of her, and with it, questions followed. Derek was still being poisoned but how? She surveyed his room again. Nothing looked out of order, and, to her knowledge, she had been the only other person in there. Except the person on Julia's staff that left food and water for the pair of them, in the *locked* rooms.

Anger turned to blind rage. She knew she had to channel her emotions into something constructive and she knew the perfect outlet. Siobhan gathered what she needed from his room, grabbed his key, locking Derek inside. She charged through the corridors with furious purpose and determination.

She rounded the corner past the conference room and down to the gym. She yanked the door at the end of the hallway open, marching past a handmaiden who failed to stop Siobhan from shoving the double doors to Julia's private quarters open.

Julia, Vena, Luther, and Alder sat at a table in the center of the room. No one was exactly startled as Siobhan entered and she was sure it was because Luther heard her coming.

"Your Sovereign, I'm sorry… I tried to stop her…" the handmaiden apologized, cutting a glare at Siobhan.

"It's alright Nara," Julia smiled softly at the younger woman. Nara turned and returned to her post in the outer room. Julia faced Siobhan scowling softly, "What is it, child?"

Siobhan glared at the four, "I'm so glad the strongest of the Hidden are here having tea while Daria is running rampant right under their damn noses. I'm thinking Derek and I would have been better off on our own… at least we have each other's backs."

She tossed the empty mug with the remnants of the detox herbs on the table. Julia's face turned white, yet her eyes remained fixed on Siobhan.

"What's this?" Vena asked.

Alder picked up the cup and smelled the leftover contents, "Ach! That stinks… What is it?"

Julia drew a shaking breath and swallowed hard, "Subane."

"Subane? Why would anyone…" Alder wondered aloud until the realization came over the group. Alder, Luther, and Vena threw themselves out of their seats, drew their weapons, and took defensive postures around Julia.

"Relax!" Siobhan's voice rose over the commotion. "She isn't here. At least, I don't think she is."

Captain Vena holstered her pistol and leaned down to a still very ashen and still very shaken Julia.

"What is it?" she asked the Sovereign softly.

Julia's eyes darted back up to Siobhan then again to Vena, "Please check on Derek… I need to know he's safe."

Vena began to move toward the door when Siobhan stepped in front of her, blocking her exit.

"He's fine.... resting for about an hour. I've got him locked in his room," she said flatly.

Vena turned back and looked at Julia for approval to which Julia nodded. She then moved back to a protective stance behind Julia's chair.

"How would she have gotten in?" Luther asked.

Alder shook his head fervently, his long hair whipped as he did, "No way. We have Brethren all along the perimeter of this complex, not to mention sentinels a mile beyond. No way she got in here."

Siobhan reached into the back pockets of her jeans and pulled out two empty disposable plastic water bottles and tossed those on the table next to the cup. She carefully looked each person in the eyes as she waited for a response but the four remained silent. Siobhan was quickly growing weary of what she perceived as underlying and unspoken secrets that she feared would get her and Derek killed.

"He was poisoned. And it's probably been going on the entire time we've been here," she cut harshly. "Smell it."

"Impossible," Luther said with an air of factual audacity.

"Smell it!" Siobhan demanded.

Alder reached out and took one of the bottles, opened the lid, and sniffed the remaining contents. His nose curled in repulsion, as he swished the contents examining them closely.

"That isn't water. And it smells like soured blood," He tossed the bottle back on the table and slapped Luther on the shoulder. "Want to check it too?"

"Unnecessary. I smelled it as soon as it was opened," Luther sniffed the air as if getting a rancid stench out of his nose.

A commotion could be heard in the outer room again. The hand-maiden Nara was heard clearly telling the person they wouldn't be allowed to enter. Siobhan turned in time to see Derek's tall frame walk through the large double doors. Nara stood behind him, obviously frustrated but just as quickly left the room when Julia motioned her out.

"I'm pretty sure what she's saying is that the call is coming from inside the house," Derek said dryly.

Color flushed back into Julia's face and her eyes lit as Derek strode in. "Oh! My child! Siobhan was telling us what happened... I am so sorry. We'll find the culprit immediately. Captain! Luther! Alder! Search the complex. Account for everyone," her voice again strong and commanding.

All three Forhelien swept quickly from the room.

The hours clicked by as the Forhelien searched every inch of the building and interrogated everyone inside. Siobhan and Derek sat anxiously at the large table waiting on the return of Casius and Alder who were sent out with members of the Brethren to track down Daria's exact location.

Julia had given clear orders that they always needed eyes on Daria and Alexis and there would be no exceptions. She also ordered Siobhan and Derek were now to be armed at all times. Casius and Vena assisted them in the armory and provided both with the blessed bullets for the guns they would now carry. The pair already paced the entire expanse of the safe house waiting for the werewolves, so they decided to sit. Siobhan wriggled uncomfortably in her chair.

"You, okay?" Derek asked.

She chuckled softly as she tried to get comfortable, "Yeah. It's just this gun is in a place that is a little *too* friendly."

Derek, who felt as if he had not smiled in weeks, burst into roaring laughter. The sound of his raucous joy bled over to Siobhan, and she couldn't help but also succumb to his amusement. It felt so good to laugh because neither had cause to do it in days. They guffawed and snorted until they were both in tears, their ribs aching with suppressed snickers.

Siobhan took a long deep breath and wiped the last of the trickles from her eyes, "Did you ever think in a million years that *this* is where you would be in your life?"

"You mean fighting a supernatural being in a room full of supernatural beings? Or just running for my life, generally speaking?" Derek chuckled a little more.

"How is any of this real?" she giggled more. "I mean," she motioned around her incredulously.

"Right?!" Derek responded matching her disbelief.

They both fell silent, and Siobhan laid her head on the table. Derek continued to watch her as she closed her eyes momentarily. His heart ached that he had seemingly pulled her into this world with him. He never wanted her to be in danger. But again, he thought, *he* may already be dead if it weren't for her. He sat, watching her, thinking about how she had always taken care of him.

He remembered back to their first meeting in that training classroom. She sat in the back so she could see everything going on in the room around her. Her auburn hair was much shorter then, and it hung right at her shoulders. He walked in, scanning the classroom with a burning desire not to sit up at the front. Apparently, Siobhan recognized the look and motioned to him that there was a seat open next to her. He graciously took it and thanked her sincerely.

That was their beginning. Just a small gesture of kindness that led to the best and most loyal friend Derek ever knew. He couldn't think of a single instance where he couldn't count on her. Theo had let him down a lot of times; especially if there was a girl involved. But Siobhan could be counted on even in her worst times.

When the relationship with Paul ended, Derek assumed she would want to take some time to get herself together. Reevaluate her life and set it back in order. But the day after Paul moved out of her apartment, there she was, making coffee and scheduling appointments. He still wasn't sure what he had done in a past life to deserve such a person in this one.

"Would you stop staring at me?" Siobhan broke the silence, her eyes still closed.

"No, I won't," Derek said as a matter of fact, and his heart started to race. There was so much he wanted to say to her and so many things he should have already said.

"Von..." he began.

She lifted her head, "Yeah?"

"Thanks for everything," he said with a deeply held breath.

"Oh... Uhm, well... you're welcome...?" she answered with feigned confusion that masked a pang of disappointment.

"I'm serious. Thank you from the bottom of my heart... I wouldn't be alive right now without you. You're pretty amazing," he declared.

Siobhan turned away from him, looking everywhere except for his face. She began pinching the skin between her finger and thumb to stop the inevitable. She wanted just by will alone to stop it. But a single tear began to fall down her cheek as she hung her head to hide it from him.

"Hey," he said gingerly, reaching out to brush the tear from her face, "I hate it when you cry."

His fingers were strong and gentle against her face, and she leaned into them. She grinned softly, "I know."

His hand lingered on her cheek for several more moments. Heat rose from Siobhan's feet, through her abdomen, and into her face. Derek dropped his hand to her neck as he leaned toward her. Just as he did, Casius swung open the large doors that led to the hallway.

"There you are!" he called. "We have an update."

***

It only took five minutes for the group to gather around the ornate table. Julia sat in her usual place at the head looking unusually anxious. "Tell us Casius, what you've found?"

"We now know where Daria is hiding. She and Alexis have moved to what they *feel* is a more secure location, a warehouse along North Channel Avenue. They have Succubae, a few demons, and other Rogues guarding the perimeter. Nothing we can't handle," Casius said confidently.

"Also," Casius hesitated, "She is starting to show with child."

Derek wanted to vomit in his mouth.

"Not to worry my child," Julia patted his hand, "We still have several days before she's ready to birth."

"Demons?" Vena asked in disbelief.

"I know," Casius nodded, "I was surprised too."

"Why is that?" Derek wondered out loud.

Luther's baritone voice could almost be felt, "Because demons hate the Succubae. And Succubae don't usually align themselves with any-one. I wonder how she has amassed such a following."

"She thinks she'll have a right to the seat soon, brother. You know how power changes perspective. She's conned others into following her in her little war," Silas grumbled.

"Ew... Demons," Zhaar spoke for the first time in days.

"My sentiments exactly," Abhainn nodded.

"What other Rogues?" asked Julia.

Casius looked from Zhaar to Silas then to his own brother. He squirmed in his seat and looked uncharacteristically uncomfortable. The whole room knew he didn't want to answer.

"Tell them, brother," Alder urged.

All eyes watched Casius as he took a breath, "I saw Touma...and." Another breath. "Varsa and Allion."

Hearing the names spoken brought about visceral responses from several at the table. Zhaar's eyes narrowed to near slits and his bright white hair turned a deep shade of blood red. Silas and Luther hissed loudly. Siobhan immediately was curious to know who these people were and why their names elicited such hatred, but as she opened her mouth to ask, Casius caught her eye and shook his head in warning. She quickly assumed that these were topics that were still very raw and decided against pushing the point. Derek also took the hint from Casius and remained quiet.

"What do we do now?" Siobhan asked delicately.

"We'll follow through with the plan as scheduled... There's no reason to wait now. Daria has made it very clear her intentions and we just simply cannot allow her to continue with her treachery," Julia replied.

"Your Sovereign, I suggest we change the plan just a little. We make our move in three days' time. This should allow for a false sense of security before we attack...let her think she's won. It will also give us time to assess the involvement of the Rouges and others," Vena suggested. "We need to know how she's convinced her own sworn enemies to take up her cause."

While everyone seemed to agree with Vena, Julia sat quietly contemplating the options. In the end, she knew that Vena was right, they needed Daria to think she was safe and the birth of the Chirion would take place as she planned.

"So be it."

14

—·—

The cinder block wall room was freshly painted with soft hues of gray and blue. A small, pillowy sectional was placed in the far-left corner while the opposite wall hosted a large four-poster bed made of exotic wood that was fitted with navy silk sheets and a comforter. A bassinet placed next to it was dwarfed in comparison, but it was no less exquisite, and the entire room was scattered with a variety of pillows and blankets.

Daria stared out the still dingy window at the water and cradled her growing belly, "Shhhh...little one... rest now, your time is coming soon."

"Miss?" the young redhead asked softly.

Daria turned, her smile sweet as she rubbed her bump, "Yes pet?"

"You wanted to see me?"

"Ahh yes, Asha," Daria replied as her candied demeanor turned quietly malevolent.

"Alexis has a job for you tonight... there is a very special guest we will be hosting soon. We need to make our preparations. Can you please make sure we are successful? I just can't go out right now in my... *condition.*"

"Of course, miss," Asha nodded, and smiled confidently, turning to leave.

"Oh, and pet?" Daria added.

"Yes?"

As the younger succubus turned back to face her, Daria grabbed her by the throat and threw her against the wall, pinning her. Daria's eyes seemed to flash blue flames as she came close to the young woman's ear to whisper harshly, "Do not fail me this time. There will be no place in my rule for incompetence."

She pulled back, looking the redhead in the eye, "Understand, yes?"

The younger succubus nodded, and Daria released her. She crossed back to the window and resumed speaking softly to her womb.

15

—·—

Derek stretched slowly as he woke from a troubled sleep; if sleep is even what it could've been called. He was anxious to end this living nightmare and didn't know if he would make it three more days of waiting. He showered and dressed quickly then went next door to see if Siobhan was awake.

He tapped softly on her door before he spoke, "Von...hey, you up?"

No answer. He knocked a little louder but received the same result. He tried the door, and it swung open wide.

"Von?" he looked around and noticed the room was empty.

'Did she go to breakfast already?'

Derek made his way down the hallway, turning into the conference room where the early meal was being served. As with every morning, a variety of food items were laid out buffet-style on tables along one wall, with a beverage station situated in the corner. He noticed Casius, Alder, and Vena were sitting together eating but there was still no Siobhan.

Casius looked up and smiled as Derek approached, "Good morning, friend."

Derek who was noticeably distracted managed a, "Morning," in return followed by, "Have any of you seen Siobhan?"

The trio looked quizzically at each other and shook their heads collectively.

"Have you tried the gym?" asked Alder.

"I just came from the gym, she wasn't there," Vena responded, as she dug into a bowl of oatmeal.

Derek frowned.

"Where could she have run off to?" he said as he headed for the gym anyway.

It took him less than three minutes to determine if she wasn't in the gym or the armory. His brow continued to furrow deeply as he returned it was then the panic began to set in.

"Did you find her?" Vena asked.

Derek shook his head furiously which caused Alder and Casius to noticeably bristle.

"Find the Sovereign," Alder growled to Vena. "Casius..."

"I'm headed to the security room," he yelled over his shoulder at his brother on his way out of the heavy double doors.

Within a few short minutes, the room was full of Forhelien and Brethren chatting in small groups waiting for Julia to arrive. Derek, who returned to Siobhan's room to search for any clues as to where she could be, made his way back to the enormous wooden table through the crowd. He found Alder, Casius, Captain Vena, Abhainn, Luther, Silas, and Zhaar gathered tightly near the head of the table. They were speaking in hushed tones over a tablet that was propped where they all could view it. Derek watched in horror as the scene played out in full color on the screen.

He saw Siobhan dressed in gray sweatpants and an oversize AC/DC tee shirt. Her long auburn hair was tied in a loose knot at the back of her head. The cameras followed her as she walked barefoot down each hallway until she came to a heavy steel door that Derek recognized led to the outside. He watched in astonishment as she pushed the door open and stepped out into the darkness.

The camera view changed, and Siobhan was seen speaking to an elf standing guard on the outside of the door. The sentry nodded at her and proceeded on his patrol. Siobhan walked halfway across the expansive parking lot. Another camera angle came into view. Siobhan continued walking to the edge of the lot where a small group of trees could be seen. She stopped and tilted her head as if listening intently to something out of frame. Movement is seen as another woman departs the cover of the trees and walks up to Siobhan, handing her a bottle of water. Siobhan drains the bottle and drops it to the ground. She takes the other woman's hand and is led to the foliage, disappearing into the night.

Derek stood in shock as the video ended abruptly. Rage and fear began to build inside him, and he clenched his teeth and fists.

"What the fuck is that?" he said, his voice so enraged he could barely breathe.

The small group of Forhelien became unnaturally quiet, each waiting for the other to respond.

"I'm sorry, brother…it looks as though she was taken," Vena explained softly.

"How!? How exactly did this happen?" he responded as calmly as he could maintain. He knew at any minute he was ready to explode.

"Fuck!"

"Derek," Luther eased, "You must keep your head. Don't allow your emotions to rule you right now."

It was the first time since they met that either vampire had called him by his name or spoken so respectfully to him. It caught him a little off guard.

"It is good advice, my child."

Derek spun around to see Julia standing right behind him, her sudden appearance also knocking him off-center.

Instead of her usual flowing gowns, she was dressed head to toe in full black tactical gear. Her greying hair normally left loose down her back was pulled back firmly in a bun and she carried two handguns in a tight-fitting shoulder holster that clipped around her small waist.

Her voice became large, "Please! Let us have some quiet here!"

Everyone in the room became hushed with the Forhelien and Derek taking seats around the table.

"Thank you," Julia showed her appreciation to the group as she sat at the head of the table.

Once everyone had found their placement, Julia remained quiet for a moment with her eyes closed and her hands clasped in front of her; she looked like a statue of someone praying. She sat motionless for what seemed like a lifetime, and no one stirred around her. She slowly raised her head and purposefully looked at each person around the table. Derek thought Julia looked somehow older than she did two days prior. The gray in her hair seemed to deepen overnight.

After she laid her eyes on the final person, she took a long, slow breath, "I have been ruling the Hidden for more years than I care to admit," she began.

"I have had the privilege of being a part of guiding our world through some of our most challenging times since the Great Treaty. I have watched many of you move up the ranks from the Brethren to the Forhelien personally. I have also watched many of our brothers and sisters in the Forhelien and Brethren fall in battles much like this one."

She hung her head again slightly, speaking softly, "I still feel the pain of those losses."

"But" her voice stronger again, "We must move forward and hope that we honor those we have lost with honorable actions. This fight is honorable. We have lived under the rule of the Great Treaty for hundreds of years... it guides our actions and reminds us that no matter our caste of being, we are all of the same matter...we have a common goal."

"The Succubae refuse to be civil. They have had the opportunity at every turn to join with us for a stronger Hidden. They collectively choose to refuse peace efforts, they collectively choose to spit in the face of our olive branches, and they collectively choose to enact chaos, violence, and acts of terror over our society and the human collective. Because of this, our actions are honorable."

The powerful statement hung in the air as the sound of heavy fists pounded on the large table in solidarity. Julia nodded to Captain Vena to continue speaking.

"As you all know, our human sister Siobhan has been taken. We have reviewed the video and it looks as though she was poisoned. We have identified the traitor in our midst as another succubae named Asha. We believe she is the one that slipped the diti'litro from the succubus to Derek in his water and we believe she has done the same to our sister," Vena spoke with authority.

Fury began to build in Derek again and Casius laid his large hand on Derek's shoulder, squeezing firmly. Derek maintained his calm.

"Our revised plan from yesterday to wait three days to move on the Succubae compound has changed. The decision has been made to move on the Succubae camp at first light," Vena continued as she strolled around the room.

"We will not give this succubus any mercy. We will not stand for this insurrection any longer. The Forhelien target is Daria and Alexis. Brethren, you will take down any Succubae that stand in the way of our mission. Capture the Rogues if you can. Do we understand our orders?" she stopped pacing and waited.

The units called out in one voice, "Gia lo-xa!"

Captain Vena looked around the room one last time before ordering, "Dismissed!"

Within moments, the room was cleared of everyone except Julia, Casius, and Derek. Casius, still holding on to Derek's shoulder, gave him one final squeeze and released his grip. As he let go, Derek's rage returned as if that constraint was the only thing holding it back.

"Son of a bitch! Is she serious!? Siobhan was poisoned. Like me? How is that possible? I didn't think Daria's venom worked on a woman?" Derek thundered, throwing himself out of the chair.

"My child..." Julia began.

"Goddamn it! Stop! I'm tired of being lied to and most of what you say is half-truths. I *know* there is something you still aren't telling me," he railed on Julia. "But you..." he looked at Casius, "Can you explain this to me?"

Julia hung her head, deciding she wouldn't argue.

"She wasn't given the diti'litro from Daria, most likely it came from Alexis," Casius told him. "Do you recognize the other woman, Asha?"

Derek took a deep breath and nodded, "Yeah, she brought food to us one night. She said she was one of your handmaidens. But she wasn't the same one that came to me in my room...where is that one?"

Casius sighed, "It's only been Asha...succubae can mess with your head, man. They can make you believe anything... it's in their venom. Daria can cook up any scenario and transmit it to you through her poison... Asha's just her delivery girl...a lackey."

"And Asha was never my handmaiden," Julia remarked carefully. "There's no end to the deceit."

Derek glared at her.

"How did Siobhan get outside, and no one noticed? Who's that elf she was talking to?" Derek interrogated.

"I spoke to Aldon myself. He said she told him she needed fresh air and would only go as far as the building's corner.... He counseled against it, but because neither of you are prisoners, he allowed it. A mistake for which he's been reprimanded," Casius replied pointedly.

"What about this *capture the Rouges* bullshit?" Derek asked.

Casius took a deep breath, "There *are* members of the hidden that've chosen to follow other darker beings.... sometimes under duress but most of the time because they are traitorous assholes.

"Casius..." Julia warned.

"All due respect Sovereign, this is no time for pleasantries. Touma, Varsa, and Allion are traitors, no matter how you cut it. Capturing them will make no difference... Touma sold out Zhaar, her own brother to a demon and it nearly got him killed... And no one in the vampire courts believes that Varsa and Allion are anything but *traitre*. They'd have a price on their heads if it didn't go against the Great Treaty. As it stands, they've been disowned," Casius said as a matter of fact.

"Well said brother," Alder added as he walked briskly through the door to the common room.

Julia sighed, "You're probably right Casius."

"Goddamn it! Fuck!" Derek slammed his fist on the table in a final fit of overwhelming emotion.

"Derek, we understand your frustration..." Alder tried to calm him.

Derek's face scowled in rage, and he pointed his finger at Alder.

"No... You don't...this is *my* fault. I brought her into this," Derek thundered. "I'm responsible for her."

"C'mon. You can't believe that" Casius countered. "Siobhan doesn't strike me as someone who is easily told what to do. You didn't *do* anything."

Derek's anger was palpable as it filled the room.

"We *will* get her back brother," Alder affirmed, motioning for Casius to follow him leaving Derek and Julia alone.

"My child," Julia said softly.

"Siobhan came with you because she is as loyal to you as you are to her. I sense the feelings you have for each other are very deep, whether you choose to admit them or not. I understand that you are frustrated with me, and I want to explain everything to you, but this is *not* the time. I promise, as soon as we have Siobhan back and Daria is put away, we'll have a nice long talk," Julia rose from her seat and walked quietly out of the room leaving Derek completely alone.

16

Siobhan's eyes fluttered, struggling to open. Light poured into the small room from several meager glass windows that lined the upper wall. Her body felt heavy, and her head was pounding. She rubbed her eyes over and over to quell the blurriness, but nothing seemed to help. Through their fuzziness, she could make out an old wrought iron bed with a thin mattress placed on top. She could feel the cold, rough concrete of the floor on her legs and back and noticed the walls were painted cinder block bricks. She pushed herself to a sitting position, rubbing her cloudy eyes once more, this time the room came into better focus.

The space was painted floor-to-ceiling dull battleship gray and it reminded her of a prison cell than an actual room. Using the bed as support, she pulled herself upright and her stomach lurched from the throbbing pain in her head. Siobhan stumbled across the floor and caught herself with the door.

'*What did I drink*?' she thought.

"No," she whispered softly to herself, "I didn't have a drink."

She tried the doorknob and realized quickly that it was locked from the outside.

"Damn," she whispered again.

Suddenly, she heard a commotion on the other side of the weighty door and backed up quickly. As she did, she rammed the back of her knees on the bed which promptly sat her down hard on the sparse mattress. The lock on the door made a loud *CLACK* as it was released, and the door swung in slowly.

Daria stood grinning at Siobhan, "Well, well, well. Looks like I've caught me a little bird."

Siobhan glared hard at the succubus, "What do you want, bitch?"

"Such ill manners... Tsk, tsk, tsk. I guess Julia didn't rub off on you. She has always been such a stickler for polite repartee," Daria remarked feigning distaste.

"I asked you a question," Siobhan demanded, trying to stand without stumbling. She refused to let Daria see her weakened.

"Oh, little bird, you're in no shape to be asking questions or making demands... it's rude," Daria stated with an edge of warning in her voice.

"It's also rude to kidnap someone, poison them, and hold them, prisoner," Siobhan retorted.

"Ah, yes. Well, little bird, you may be correct there... But you see, I have a very important job for you to do. Can you guess what that is?" the succubus inched closer to Siobhan.

Siobhan closed the gap between them and stood centimeters from Daria.

"What's that?" she said through clenched teeth.

Daria smiled her wide, oily grin showing all of her white as-stone teeth, "You're my bait."

Without a warning of pretense, Siobhan had her hands around Daria's throat. Daria countered quickly, grabbing Siobhan's throat, and threw her against the wall with force. Before Siobhan knew it, the woman she recognized as Asha and a vampire had her held against the wall by her arms; she couldn't move. She could only stare in horror as Alexis entered the room, reaching out his hands to cup her face. She heard Daria's gleeful giggles and felt an electric pulse before the room turned dark again.

17

—·—

D erek sat on the bed in the still darkness. He listened intently trying to sense any sound, even the movement of air, but it seemed the world balanced in placidity. The bed's coverings were still unmade, the hills and valleys of cotton forming shadows across its length. He sat for so long in the black that his eyes had adjusted perfectly to the lack of light. He could see the duffle bag sitting in the leather office chair just across from him, some of its contents spilling over the seat. He could also clearly see the running shoes at the foot of the bed that were eggplant purple in the daylight.

He sniffed the air and noticed, for the first time he thought, the scent of her perfume; a soft mix of light musk and sweetness, like vanilla or fresh cotton candy. He reached over, picking up a faded, maroon hoodie that hung on the post of the bed, and breathed her scent deep into his lungs. The more he became aware of her smell, the more his heart ached. The more his heart ached, the more the rage grew.

He spent most of the day getting armed for the upcoming raid on the Succubae compound. Vena had one final briefing with the Forhelien and the Brethren separately and Derek made sure he was present for both. Even though Casius and Alder had encouraged him to eat heartily at dinner *'For strength!'*, he just couldn't stomach anything.

He was angry and wanted vengeance. He spent most of his evening pacing around the inside and outside of the building until he could walk it blindfolded.

He first retired to his own room and found that sleep eluded him. He thought that maybe looking for clues again in Siobhan's room would somehow abate his anxiety, but he couldn't have been more wrong. There was nothing there that would help him get her back. Derek took one more look at the room and grabbed the tactical bag he placed next to the door. He left the room and closed the door quietly.

'*Twenty-three, twenty-four, twenty-five, twenty- six, turn,*'he thought to himself as he walked stealthily in the pitch black of a hidden hallway.

He had spent the day memorizing every hall and door in the enormous building and now his efforts were paying off. He also watched the Brethren guard and their patrols around the borders of the complex. He knew that there were a few hallways that only the Forhelien and Brethren used as their own and that these wouldn't be as heavily surveyed. He honestly didn't think they would be occupied at all at night and as it turned out, he was right.

'*Thirty-five, thirty-six, thirty-seven,*' he continued to mentally count his steps.

In the near distance, a faint square of light could be seen as he moved silently through the passage. He moved more quickly now, careful not to make his footfalls heavy. When he got close enough, he reached out to feel the cool metal of the door handle and the frosty tempered glass at eye level. He twisted the knob softly and pulled the door open slowly. A small gust of cool wind blew in his face as he looked out just enough to check for a patrol guard. When he was satisfied there was no one around, Derek slipped out into the night.

Derek's quiet actions of watching and listening to the previous day paid off. After stealing one of the Brethren's vehicles, he made short work of finding the warehouse where Daria and Alexis were hiding. It was a short ten-minute drive over to the Willamette side of the peninsula. Presumably, Siobhan would be there too, along with a collection of Daria's own guards.

He parked about a mile down the road so as not to alert anyone to his presence too soon. He assumed Daria would have a similar protection detail the Forhelien and Brethren set up for Julia which included sentries a few blocks beyond the border of the building. He also suspected that there would be guards walking the grounds and needed to figure out how to get close enough to time their movements so he could slip through. Derek sat in the dark van and considered his options. His priority was to find Siobhan and make sure she was safe; then he would destroy Daria.

Siobhan. The mere thought of her name sent a pang to his heart. His mind raced with memories and emotions that connected him to her as if he could somehow reach out through space and time to tell her that he was coming. One rushing thought made him stop cold and a deluge of realization poured over him. A thought, that the more he contemplated, the more his own breath stopped short in his chest. That one thought, that one insight...that he loved Siobhan.

He had always *loved* her. She was the closest friend he had, but now he knew it was more than that kind of platonic love. It was more than a fleeting schoolboy crush on someone he admired at the moment or a lustful wistfulness for a passing woman on the street. This was a stronger feeling than he ever had for any of the women he had dated or been with in his entire life. He was full, with every cell in his body, completely *in love* with her.

He had no hesitation in finally admitting it to himself now. The more thoughts and memories that rushed his mind of her, the more he realized the exact moment he fell for her. But for some reason, he deliberately chose to ignore them. Then, he talked himself out of it. After so much time passed, he lied to himself about his feelings and did it for so long, that he actually believed they weren't true. But somehow, Julia knew it; apparently, it was obvious to her. What an asshole he was for not telling her or acting on it before. His stomach fell as he realized now, he may lose her. As this final thought solidified with him, he became more determined, and a fierce fire raged inside him. He had never felt this way for anyone in his life and he knew he never would feel the same for anyone else. He would get Siobhan back or die trying.

He pulled the tactical bag across his chest and unholstered his handgun. He jogged quickly along the empty road using the trees that lined it as coverage along the way. Deciding that a dark alley would allow for better concealment, he raced quickly toward the succubae hold. Within a few moments, he was close enough to see the lone building that backed up against the riverfront. Hiding beneath a tractor-trailer he watched as two guards walked along the top of the building. From his vantage point, he could see there was only one person walking the lot on the ground. Three sentries total; those were odds he could play.

Derek continued to zig and zag between large trailers and patches of trees, always keeping in the shadows until he was at the edge of the sidewalk that ran in front of the squat building. He hid in the deep shadow of a large tree until he could see the guard on the ground around the corner of the building. He moved quickly across the small parking lot and hugged close to the building, waiting for the guard to come back around the corner. As he did, Derek was ready for him.

He grabbed the Incubus by the collar of his coat, punching hard into his throat, making it impossible for him to yell out. Derek's fist gave two more blows to his face, knocking him unconscious. He found the zip-tie handcuffs and secured the incapacitated incubus to the building's plumbing system. The shadows on that side of the building were so dark, that Derek knew it would be morning before the man would be found.

Derek could hear the muffled footsteps of the roof guards as he made his way to a door on the side of the building. Using the keys he took from the incubus, he found the one that unlocked the door, slipping inside. Once inside he found a choice to be made go left, further into the darkness, or turn right and follow the hall to the glow of soft light. Before he chose, he listened closely for any voices but heard nothing. Closing his eyes, he let instinct choose; he moved toward the light.

He was careful to keep his footfalls soft as he snuck along the narrow corridor. He came to a large room filled with machinery that looked as though it hadn't been used in some time. Even though he didn't know what was made there, he was sure he was in an old manufacturing facility. The air around him smelled damp and old. The light he had been following turned out to be a caged overhead fixture that swung slightly, and it made the hair on the back of Derek's neck rise. He wasn't alone.

Cold laughter echoed throughout the vast space, and he immediately recognized the chill of the maniacal shriek. Raising his eyes, Daria appeared standing on the catwalk overhead. Instinctually, Derek moved back down the hallway just in time to see a knife blade fly by his head. He turned to see the pale, thin face of a woman growling in frustration at him.

The resemblance to Zhaar was uncanny. Touma and Zhaar carried the same sharp facial features and her eyes narrowed much in the same way Zhaar's had at the mention of her name. Her hair wasn't the stark white that her brother preferred, but a very bright pink hanging in sweeping curls.

As she pulled back to take aim again, Derek raised his gun and fired. The bullet caught Touma in the shoulder and she screamed in pain. Derek sensed more movement behind him, turning just in time to see another incubus rushing toward him. Without hesitation, Derek shot again, this time catching the incubus directly in the forehead. The incubus' head flew back violently, and he dropped to the ground.

Daria screamed in a murderous rage, "No! Get him! Stop him now!"

Derek ran toward the stairwell that led to the catwalk but before he could take his first leap on the riser four hands grabbed onto his shoulders and yanked him back painfully. He twisted out of the grasp of one set of hands and shoved the attacker's head hard into the block wall. He began fighting hard with the other attacker. He raised his gun to take another shot, but it was knocked forcefully out of his grip. Blows landed hard on his face and his rib cage as Derek traded punches with the unknown assailant.

For what seemed like several minutes, Derek's rage powered him as he landed an uppercut and cross, knocking the other man off his feet. Bloodied, Derek turned back toward the stairwell, climbing the steps two at a time. He reached the place where he saw Daria last and looked around; she was gone.

Derek stood there for a moment, catching his breath. He looked down to clearly see the two incubae he had just fought writhing on the floor below. Derek froze just as he felt the electric pulse run down his face and Daria's malicious laughter fading in his ears.

18

— • —

Derek's eyes flashed open, and he sat up quickly. The dim light shining in the room showed him the sun was setting. How long had he been out? His legs felt like jelly as he tried to stand from the old metal-framed bed. He could still feel Daria's laughter ringing in his ears. A sound that sickened and enraged him at the same time. He knew that he needed to get out of that room and find Siobhan. His head pounded softly as he stumbled his way to the thick metal door in front of him. To his surprise, he pulled on the handle, and it opened smoothly. Poking his head out, he looked around but saw no one and he slipped quietly out.

The light was changing faster, and the shadows morphed into abstract silhouettes along the walls and floor. Derek, careful to stay within the safe confines of those shadows, moved quickly along the length of the hallway. The path made a sharp turn right and opened up into a large marble room covered in what he could only assume was very expensive artwork.

As if professionally placed, paintings of all styles hung on the walls of the large room and small spotlights were expertly placed to highlight the individual pieces. Six stone pillars were arranged symmetrically in the middle of the floor. On top of the pillars sat crystal clear glass boxes encasing various statues and treasures. Bench seats of soft, tawny leather well positioned for viewing, completed the space. Derek looked around in awe; this room could compete with any well-known museum in the country.

He made his way through the expanse, his footsteps echoing softly on the marble floor. As he exited that room, he found himself inside another filled with more artwork. He raced from showroom to showroom; all of them filled with priceless work. Finally, he came to a stairwell and stopped. His only choice was to go up since he had already searched all the rooms on this level looking for Siobhan. He sprinted the steps, two at a time again, with his long stride but only found more artwork.

'Where could she be?' he thought, frustrated. More rooms, more stairs. He raced through the entire museum until he was almost out of breath.

"Siobhan!" he yelled.

He didn't care anymore about being quiet. He didn't care that the monsters would be able to find him. The only thing that mattered was that he saw her again. He wanted to tell her he was sorry for everything and that he loved her.

'No... It's more than that,' he thought.

He was desperate to tell her that he was *in* love with her and had always been. He wanted her to know that no matter how much she pushed him away, he would always be in love with her. It was then that he heard it; just a small, muffled voice in the dark.

"Siobhan?" he whispered, becoming still so he could pinpoint the direction the noise was coming from.

Another indistinct sound. He walked around the edge of the large room until he found a small hallway almost completely hidden by a very large stone statue of a naked Grecian goddess. It only led in one direction and at its end was a heavy steel door that looked very out of place. His heart pounded in his chest and almost as hard as his head. Derek reached out his hand and opened the door.

19

Siobhan stood on the cold concrete floor and felt aged. She knew she needed to find Derek and stop all of this madness, but where was he? She crossed the long, bright marble room; her steps echoing in the empty space.

"Derek!" she shouted, and her voice carried like her footfalls. But the silence was the only answer she received.

She quickened her pace as the anxiety began to grow inside of her. He was being so foolish and irresponsible. After all that she had put him through; no, put *them* through, why did he have this sudden change of heart? It wasn't like him. When Derek made up his mind about something, that was the end of the subject. She had never, in all the years of knowing him, witnessed him acting so foolhardy.

Siobhan turned a corner and entered another dimly lit room. This room had walls of pure white and was decorated with very expensive-looking oil paintings of some noble family from many ages ago. Their muted reds, blues, and gold would have stood in stark contrast to the alabaster room, had the lights been turned on. Panic started to set in her mind as she spun around the room looking for any sign of him. She found no evidence he had been in the area and made fast for the next oak door. As she crossed the threshold into yet another sparkling room, something small caught her attention on the floor.

She stared for a long moment at the perfectly circular spot on the carpet. As if she was looking at something unrecognizable, she bent down to inspect it. She dragged her finger through the perfect droplet, and it smeared. The blood was still warm on her finger as she rubbed her shaking hands together. She rose and noticed the trail of more perfect, bright red beads along the floor.

"Derek!" she screamed.

The absence of sound around her filled her ears with a droning buzz. She pushed all of her thoughts and energy into finding him as she raced across the event-sized room. She dodged around large pillars as she followed the growing path of blood. The trail ended at yet another doorway, but this time it was smeared all over with red and she could only make out a single handprint.

It took all of Siobhan's strength to shove the heavy door open, her hands slipping on the bloody handle. The room beyond was black as pitch and it took her eyes several moments to adjust to the lack of light. When she could faintly make out shapes in the darkness, she remembered the flashlight on her phone and decided to use it to help guide her. Her hands continued to tremble as she wiped the blood on her pants and dug for it in her pocket. The tiny light lit up the room like a headlamp and she scanned her surroundings.

Stacks of boxes, paintbrushes, and other various items filled the room. She moved carefully around the piles of clutter as she continued to follow the growing blood trail. It was at that moment she saw a figure move in front of her, just out of the small lamp's reach.

"Derek?" she asked out loud as she moved the light to see in front of her. A wild, maniacal laugh began to build around her, and fear shot down her spine like an icy spear.

"Derek?" the female voice mocked as the light from Siobhan's phone moved over her and the mass at her feet.

Without hesitation, Siobhan ran toward the woman and whatever she was standing over. Falling to her knees she dropped her phone and its light reflected back from the tin ceiling, brightening the space around her. She rolled over the heavy heap of cloth to find Derek, his face absent of all color and his eyes sunken.

"Derek! Oh my God!" Siobhan cried aloud as she search him for injuries.

The woman who was now standing just out of arms reach of Derek and Siobhan laughed again wildly, "He did it to himself...poor thing. How sad!"

Siobhan's heart was racing, and she grabbed his hands to shake him. It was then that she felt the now familiar sticky thickness of blood. She looked down and found both his wrists had been cut open as a bloody box knife fell from his right hand. Siobhan looked around frantically for something to cover his wounds. Finding an old drop cloth nearby, she tore into it and wrapped the pieces around his wrists tightly.

"It's too late! He's done it! It's over...there isn't anything you can do," the woman cackled as she continued to watch Siobhan's desperate actions.

"No! It's not! Derek..." Siobhan finished tying the final knot on the bandages and reached out to hold Derek's head in her blood-covered hands. "Why...why!?"

The woman tilted her head in wonderment, staring at Siobhan, "I always knew there was something more... I should have taken that too."

It was then that Siobhan finally recognized the woman's face.

"Weasel cunt."

"That was ill-mannered," the woman chided her.

"Why did you do this? Why!?" Fresh, hot tears formed in Siobhan's eyes.

More manic laughing filled the room, "Oh, sweet Siobhan... He did it himself."

The woman touched her own face, and a look of shock crossed it.

"Oh, I'm sorry," She apologized with a sickly, sweet tone, "I forgot to take off my makeup."

With that statement, the woman reached under both ears with her hands and pulled. The skin lifted from her like a mask, and it made a sound similar to a suction cup being released. To Siobhan's horror, Daria's face appeared from beneath it.

"Well, that's better dear," her voice lyrical.

"Why? Why would you do this to him?" Siobhan's face flooded with tears as she choked on her words.

"This is what he wanted. He couldn't take it anymore...the pain was just too...much," she said dramatically, and the otherworldly laughter filled the room again.

Daria turned to leave but stopped, "I'm so glad he's made it easier on me...I hate getting my hands dirty....you seem to have something on yours."

She turned again on her heel and disappeared into the darkness.

Siobhan stared after her for several seconds as she considered following Daria. She turned her attention back to Derek and began to run her hands over his face again lovingly. The tears flowed like rivers from her eyes.

"Oh, God! Why?" she cried as she struggled to stop the bleeding.

"Why did you do this? So stupid...so...stupid," she rocked her body back and forth as her anguish became unbearable.

"What am I supposed to do now, huh? Oh, God! What am I supposed to do now!?"

The silence was again the only answer to her screams of pain.

20

— · —

Siobhan writhed in the rickety bed. Her breath was shallow as the sweat poured off her. She grappled with the blankets under her as if they were fighting back against her own body. She desperately wanted to open her eyes, but they felt like lead weights were holding them down. She fought the immediate need to vomit and instead swallowed the growing lump in her throat.

'Get up Siobhan. GET UP!' she told herself.

She lifted her heavy hands, forced her eyelids open, and carefully surveyed the room. It was almost completely dark, the only light coming from outside through the small windows above her. The room smelled damp and a little old and she thought she could hear the soft lapping of waves in the near distance.

Looking over her own body, she examined it for restraints or trauma. She was as she had been before: gray sweats and an oversize tee-shirt. She lay for another moment listening as hard as she could for any movement outside of her cell, but all was silent. She finally managed to roll to her side and lay there for a moment while the room settled and stopped spinning. Her head throbbed as though she had been beaten with a hammer, the remnants of the incubus' poison still working its way out of her system. Sitting up slowly, she placed her naked foot on the floor, and it touched something soft and human-like.

"Jesus!" Siobhan muffled a scream by covering her mouth and jumping back on the bed.

Adrenaline began to rush, and she was clear-eyed now. She leaned over the bed to find what she had stepped on, a human hand. As she looked closer and her eyes adjusted to the dark, she could see the hand led to a full body, dressed in all black lying on the floor in the middle of the room.

Siobhan moved off the bed and crept closer to the person. She could feel the treaded boots under her fingers as she made her way up the body looking for the person's identity. She reached over and tilted the man's head back toward her and realized in relief and horror that it was Derek.

"Oh my god!" she said hoarsely. She shook his shoulders and leaned over to check for breathing. It gave her some comfort when she found his pulse on his unharmed wrists and could feel his breath on her cheek.

"Derek. Derek!" she continued to shake him.

No response came.

21

The heavy door swung wide, and Derek stared in disbelief at the scene in front of him. Luther stood over Siobhan gently stroking her hair as she smiled lovingly up at him. She reached her hands up to his face, caressing it gently. Luther bared his icy white fangs in a large smile and made a purring sound from deep within. Neither of them seemed to notice Derek standing in the doorway.

"What the hell is going on?" Derek demanded as he rushed toward Luther. "Get your fucking hands off her!"

Siobhan stepped between the pair of men, hissing, "How dare you? Who are you to say who puts their hands on me?"

Derek stepped back, confused, "Von?"

Her look was cold and angry, "You left me. You said you didn't want me. You said we would never be anything, not even friends. I was the one that followed you. I would have done anything for you, but you threw me away like trash."

"Von, I never..." Derek started to speak but found his throat was like a desert.

"You did! Everyone warned me. They warned me that you would never change. But I had hope. I thought you would change your mind...then that night, in your apartment. The night of the storm. We came so close, but you pushed me away... literally. I still can't believe you put your hands on me like that," Siobhan thundered. "How dare you!"

"Von, I never touched you...you were the one that backed away. No...wait. That's not what happened." Derek was thinking out loud now, "He touched you... I made him leave...we hung out, that's it... I wanted you to feel safe."

He paced around the small room starting at Luther and Siobhan, "You told me...told me...told..."

Derek started to counter her argument but lost his thought track. His head was throbbing, and he thought the top might explode.

"Are you calling her a liar?" Luther growled softly.

Derek shook his head to clear it, "No. I..."

"I said a lot of things and there is so much more to say. It's no wonder she left you alone...You're a terrible excuse for a human," Siobhan bellowed.

"What? Who? Who left me?" Derek demanded.

Luther let out a hearty laugh that filled the room, "Pathetic."

Boom, boom, boom

Derek's head pounded.

"This. This isn't real. This is *not* real," Derek almost smiled.

Luther and Siobhan cackled wildly, and Derek turned on them. "*You* aren't real," he pointed at Luther and Siobhan.

"Neither of you. Daria stop! Get out of my fucking mind...You fucking bitch, I said STOP!" he screamed.

Luther and Siobhan faded like a mirage.

22

The sun had not begun to rise when Captain Vena made her way down the long hallway to the rooms occupied by their human guests. She rounded the corner and noticed the light fixture that hung between the doors of the two rooms was out. She stared at it with slight curiosity as she knocked on Derek's door. She became acutely aware that she heard no sound from beyond; she knocked again and was met with more silence. She turned the unlocked handle, pushed open the door, and carefully stared at the room beyond. The realization came over her suddenly; the room was empty, and Derek was gone.

Vena sprinted back through the conference space and into the security room. There she found Casius involved in an intense conversation with the Brethren guard.

"Casius!" Vena ordered and looked at the Brethren soldier, "You, out."

"Well, that was rude..." Casius stared at her.

"Derek is gone. Can you pull up the outer building footage for the last six hours?" Vena's voice carried ordered desperation.

"Damn it... You know where he went, right? Julia isn't going to like this," Casius stated as he began rewinding video feeds from outside of the safe house.

Vena sighed heavily, "He's only going to get himself and his girl-friend killed."

"Really? You think they're *together*?" Casius mused as he continued to rewind moments from that night.

"I assume so... I mean, the way they look at each other, right?" she stated as her eyes scanned over the tapes as fast as they moved onscreen.

Casius shrugged, "Lucky guy. That Siobhan is everything one would look for in a mate... I bet she's got a little were-blood in her."

Vena laughed as she continued to follow the images, "I doubt that Casius...wait! There! Stop the tape."

"Good eyes, Elf," Casius teased as he moved the video back three frames and played it forward.

It wasn't much, but in the very corner of the screen, someone dressed all in black and carrying a dark tactical bag came from behind a van and around to the driver's seat, entering the vehicle. A few seconds later, the black van left the parking area, turned right, and drove into the night.

"Damn it!" Vena exclaimed in frustration.

Casius hung his head, groaning, "I'll get the others."

***

"What do you mean he is gone?" Silas barked.

"I'm not sure what part of that you're not understanding Silas," Vena tried to temper her voice, but it was becoming more embittered.

"He did a very good job at staying out of sight of all our surveillance. Of course, it wouldn't take much for someone to time the movement of each camera or even the new guards. We weren't concerned with someone getting out, just others getting in," Casius explained.

Julia, whose face showed someone that was getting by on little to no sleep, took a long haggard breath.

"We have no time to waste," she said quietly, "We leave now."

With her words, the Forhelien sprang to action. Within ten minutes the room was filled with Forhelien, and Brethren all weighed down with a variety of weaponry and taking transport assignments. The last few days of planning had come down to this moment.

As the soldiers made their way out of the building and began piling into the armored vans, Julia stood back to take in the scene. It was one she had watched many times before and every time she prayed it would be the last. She abhorred violence but was well-prepared for it and well-trained in it. She hoped that she would be able to get Derek and Siobhan back without much bloodshed, but she knew that Daria was vengeful and wouldn't allow for any mercy by either side. Daria had always hated Julia and this scheme of hers was just the cherry on top of a decades-long war with Julia, the Order, and the Hidden.

Julia remembered her first run-in with the beautiful, blonde succubus. This was a time long before she had become Sovereign of the Hidden and didn't hold the responsibility or the tactfulness she did today. Back then, Julia was just a teenage witchling who thought she had the entirety of Hidden and human knowledge in her back pocket. She didn't know how cruel either world could really be. It was also a time when Julia had found herself completely smitten with one of the young male pages in her mother's court. They spent months exchanging flirtations and sideways glances with each other. Her mother, of course, had higher aspirations for the young Julia but tolerated the innocent dalliance at the time. It all came apart however when Daria arrived.

Daria passed herself off as a young witch when she arrived at the royal court. She was able to perform some basic parlor tricks easily.

Along with her venom, was able to fool those at the lower levels of the echelon into thinking she was just a poor, orphaned witch in need of training. As she made friends with those at higher levels, Julia became her natural competition. There was no doubt that the only child of Sovereign Rosalind would ascend to the throne and become a strong leader. These were two things that Daria desired, but she would need Julia out of the way for that to happen. There was no amount of sabotage that was beneath Daria, including the young page that was trying to steal Julia's heart.

Julia remembered the shock she felt when they found the page dead right outside her room at Arvendon. At first, all eyes looked at her in guilt at his death and it was a feeling she couldn't get rid of even now. She allowed her mind to reflect back to those days...how different her life would have been had Daria been apprehended so many years before.

"Sovereign? Ma'am..." Alder spoke to her. He had been calling to her for several moments now, "Julia?"

"Oh, Alder...I'm so sorry....I must have been..." Julia apologized.

"In another time?" Alder finished for her and looked at her with empathy. "I know all this weighs heavily on you. I know you're worried for your..."

She hissed quietly at him, looking to see that no one was within earshot, "Shht... Alder, please."

"If I may..." Alder moved around to face her and spoke softly where only she could hear, "Julia, this chess game you're playing needs to end. You're the only one that is able to see the entire board and make the moves that are necessary... except the one move you're avoiding..."

Julia sighed and smiled tiredly at him, "I'm aware, old friend. We need to make this our play now...I'll work on the other later. It's just so damn hard..." Tears started to form in the older woman's weary eyes.

Alder laid his oversize hand on her shoulder and squeezed gently. "We *will* end this with the succubus today. Just..." his eyes lay on her just as gently as his touch, "Be sure you're prepared for *every* outcome."

"Thank you, Alder," she nodded.

Alder turned sharply, returning to his post at the van that carried a group of Forhelien. Julia followed and slid into the front seat.

23

— · —

Derek sat up with a jerk, knocking Siobhan back on her butt. He looked at her in shock as she clamored back to him, "Oh my god, Von, is that you?"

"Yes… Shhhh…you have to be quiet," she hushed him.

He grabbed her by the shoulders, and pulled her to him, holding her tightly, "Son of a bitch, I thought I'd lost you."

Siobhan let out a small laugh as she was buried in his grasp, "Well, we're still locked in a cell with about a dozen monsters out there….I'm saying we're not out of the woods yet."

She pulled away and examined the noticeable damage on his face, "What the hell happened to you?"

He gave her a half grin, "A fae and three incubae…and Daria."

"Cunt."

Derek nodded, "I think she knows I'm awake. We have to hurry."

He surveyed the room.

"What are you looking for?" Siobhan asked.

"My tactical bag… it'd be stupid for them to leave it…they didn't," Derek said.

"So, we're screwed," Siobhan replied.

Derek smiled, winked at her, and pulled himself standing, "Not exactly."

He bent over carefully, reached inside his left boot, and pulled out a small, zippered pouch that looked much like a grooming kit for nails.

"What's that?" she asked.

"Something I borrowed from the Forhelien armory," he replied.

His head was still hurting, but the rampant throbbing had subsided. He reached into his right boot, pulled out the smallest handgun Siobhan had ever seen, and handed it to her. She watched as he started to unzip his pants.

"Whoa... What are you...." her voice trailed off as Derek pulled another handgun from a holster attached to the inside of his upper thigh.

"Okay Rambo," she giggled.

Derek handed the gun from his leg to Siobhan also. Walking over to the door, he unzipped the small pouch to reveal five small metal tools of differing shapes and bends. He knelt in front of the locking mechanism and began to use the lock pick kit to open the door. After several minutes, they both heard a soft *click* as the pin was released.

"Hey!" Siobhan grinned, "Great job!"

He zipped the kit up, jamming it in his pocket then turned and faced her, "We have to get you out of here... I'm going to find a way out then I'm taking Daria down. I need you to get back to the safe house. There's a black van parked about three blocks away, keys are still in it."

Siobhan was already shaking her head in vehement disapproval, "Not a chance. I'm *not* leaving you here... We're in this together... remember?"

Derek opened his mouth to disagree, but Siobhan wouldn't let him begin, "We don't have time to argue... We need a plan."

After a little discussion, Derek twisted the knob and the heavy door opened smoothly. He eyed the hallway looking for any movement. Only after he was confident they were alone, did he step out into the semi-darkness with Siobhan close behind. They crept down the narrow corridor until they came to a set of double doors and went through. They walked carefully along in silence until the sound of someone talking froze them in place. The conversation moved along the hallway, coming closer to them. They could tell it was one person, a female, and she seemed to be having a deep exchange on a phone. Derek and Siobhan backed down an adjacent hallway and hid in the shadows. As the woman came closer, both Derek and Siobhan recognized her voice; it was Asha.

"No. I said you need to find me everything I have asked for... his prince will be here in the next two days, and I will have everything perfect for my mistress."

She paused as though she were listening closely, "You will have those items here in an hour along with everything else that was requested, or you won't have my mistress to fear, but me."

The phone made an audible *beep* as she hung up. Asha still had her back turned when Siobhan grabbed her by the hair and placed her hand over her mouth. She squeezed her nose tightly and cut off her air supply with an arm lock to the neck. It was a quiet and swift movement and even took Derek by surprise. Siobhan slid Asha down to the ground and pulled her farther into the shadows of the hallway.

Leaning over Siobhan, Derek whispered hoarsely, "Why did you do that? Is she dead?"

Siobhan shook her head fiercely and looked up at Derek, pointing to Asha's feet, "No," she replied. "Just unconscious... I need her shoes."

Derek looked down and noticed that Siobhan was still barefoot as she had been when she was taken. He helped her pull the flat loafers from Asha's feet so she could wear them.

"Better?" Derek whispered.

"Much. Let's go," she nodded.

The pair continued down the hallway until they came to another door that opened into a large warehouse area. Boxes and packing materials were stacked high and scattered throughout the sizable space. The same boxy windows that were in Siobhan's cell lined the entirety of the wall to the left of the door. They could see it becoming lighter outside and heard the distant splashing of water from the river. The wall to their right was lined with bay doors every fifty feet, presumably for loading trucks. Derek motioned in the direction of the far end of the warehouse where a red door could be seen under a dimly blinking exit sign.

Siobhan nodded in agreement and followed.

24

Dozens of Brethren swarmed the succubae hideout like locusts in a drought as the dark vans screeched to a halt in the parking lot. Silas and Luther were the first Forhelien out of their vehicle and rushed to the heavy front door with blinding speed. Sweeping through the first hallway, they landed blow after crushing blow to any succubae that dared to get in their way. The first of the Brethren soldiers made their way through the path that the vampires had cut and began to clear rooms and hallways as they went. Bursts of automatic gunfire could be heard the further they pushed into the building.

Casius and Abhainn directed their attention to the second level of the complex, moving with the synchronicity of a Swiss watch. Casius moved adeptly through the corridor while Abhainn covered him, then Abhainn would advance. This graceful game of leapfrog continued until they were met with heavy gunfire from an adjacent hallway to their right.

Abhainn, caught a glimpse of their assailants as he peeked around to fire. "Son of a..." he yelled.

"Who?" Casius hollered back.

"Varsa!" Abhainn called over his shoulder.

Casius's growl could be felt as well as heard over the rapid gunfire as he pressed the speaker button on his jacket collar.

"Silas! You've got someone here to see you...get your ass up here and say hello," he yelled into the tiny microphone as he and Abhainn continued drawing fire from deep within the corridor. Within moments, Casius felt the air move behind him, turning in time to see Silas rush to his side.

"Where is she?" Silas asked with a dangerous calm.

"Just inside the third door," Abhainn yelled back at him from his own crouched position, "We're taking heavy fire, there're more in that hallway."

Casius and Silas looked around the corner simultaneously and saw a flash of hot pink hair move quickly down the hall and duck around a corner.

"Fuck," said Casius with exasperation, "Pretty sure that's Touma."

Silas continued to dart his head around the corner watching. On his third peek, Casius watched a sudden salacious grin spread across his face as Silas witnessed the shimmering appearance of Zhaar behind Touma. Zhaar's gangly body faded in like a mirage as he wrapped his long, thin arms around her body.

Touma screamed a high pitch shriek as Zhaar said, "Hello little sister."

As quickly as he had appeared, Touma and Zhaar were gone.

With one of their fighters disappearing in front of them, the remaining Succubae and their cronies started retreating further into the darkness. Silas couldn't wait any longer.

"My turn," he snarled.

"Vaarrssaaaa," Silas drew her name out, "Come out and face me...have a little bit of honor, won't you?"

"Honor? What do you know of *honor*?" Varsa called back from her hiding place. "Still taking orders from your human sorceress, I see?"

"God you're pathetic," Silas moaned as he moved from one cover to another, "You always were a spoiled brat."

Silas lunged and with a dizzying speed made his way further down the corridor, locking in on her position. Silas was a blur as he dodged around the gunfire. He popped around the corner, locking his large hand over her narrow throat. Suddenly the gun blasts stopped as the accompanying succubae retreated at the sight of the Forhelien vampire.

Varsa gagged as Silas held his grip on her, "How dare you?! I am your mother!"

"Oh, it's going to be a lovely homecoming," Silas's oily grin spread across his face once more and again with blinding speed, dragged Varsa out of the building by her neck.

Both the Forhelien and Brethren fought against the Succubae forces for nearly twenty minutes before finding Daria's nursery. Unfortunately, the room was empty, and they continued moving forward with their search for the nest's leader. Zhaar had reappeared and again stood with his fellow soldiers.

Casius acknowledge him first, "Where's Touma?"

"Back in the Hidden...I have placed her in a confinement cell at Arvendon. She is very unhappy," his voice ethereal and strained.

Casius nodded his approval "One of these days Zhaar, you're going to have to teach us how you get into the Hidden without a doorway."

He then pressed the button on his radio microphone, "I need a call out... Captain Vena, I need a location on you and The Lady."

"Affirmative Casius... We have several wounded Brethren, all Forehelien accounted for...I've sent the injured back to the Hidden for treatment. Right now, Lady, Alder, I, and several others are making our way around to the back of the building... we believe we can gain access within a few minutes," Vena was breathing heavily through the radio as if she were running.

Casius made a motion with his hand, directing Abhainn and Zhaar to head toward the back of the building.

"We're headed your way," he replied to Captain Vena.

The trio raced down hallways and was met with surprisingly little resistance.

"Where is everyone?" Abhainn asked.

Casius, who still hadn't broken a sweat, stopped suddenly, turning his head to listen. Abhainn was right. They ran into several groups of Brethren, but most of them either had captives or were standing guard.

"We keep moving," he said, "We still don't have a location on Daria."

The group moved through the building with growing speed. They rounded around the corner of the final hallway that led to the warehouse and was met with sudden snaps gunfire from the remaining Succubae. They were positioned in front of the dual swinging doors that led directly into the warehouse beyond. Casius, Zhaar, and Abhainn looked at each other in shock.

"Guess we know where the rest went," Abhainn snarked.

"She must be in there. No other reason for that many people to be locked down in one area. Zhaar, can you shift in?" Casius asked as he continued covering Abhainn, allowing the elf to reload his weapon.

Zhaar's usually soft voice carried in the corridor, "No. Demons are blocking the egress."

"Damn it! We should've done this during the high moon...it'd be easier for me that way," Casius growled and pressed the microphone again.

"Vena, we've got a sweet mix of hostiles here. It's going to be a minute before we'll be through...you're going to have to get in that warehouse. Daria is in there."

25

—·—

Derek and Siobhan began to make their way across the expanse of the enormous warehouse, dodging behind stacks of boxes in an attempt to make it difficult for anyone who may be looking for them. Derek had a feeling Daria knew they had escaped the cell and were making their way out. Suddenly, Siobhan gave out a loud guttural yell and Derek turned back to find Alexis holding her by her long hair. Derek froze as Alexis' free hand threatened to connect with Siobhan's face.

"No!" Derek yelled, "Don't!"

A familiar cackling echoed through the expanse and moved closer to Derek. Daria's wintery blue eyes glowed from the darkness.

She slinked out of the shadows like a snake with its prey cornered, "Oh, Derek my love. What's the matter? Afraid she'll like it?"

Derek drew his gun on Daria and pointed it at her head.

"He touches her, you die," his voice was calm and direct.

"Ohhh!" Daria giggled wildly, "They want to play! Look, Alexis! My sweet Derek likes games!"

"No game Daria... Let her go. She doesn't have anything to do with this," Derek's voice remained even.

"But, my love, she does... You both are playing the same role," she said coyly.

"What is that?" Derek demanded, his gun never moving from its target.

Daria rolled her eyes in fake exasperation, "Bigger fish lover. Bigger fish. But, enough with that boring cat and mouse game... It has become so drab. I'm ready for a new one."

"Me too. Let's see if you can catch this bullet," Derek gave her an evil grin.

Siobhan yelled again, falling to her knees as Alexis pulled on her hair tighter. Daria's eyes were filled with quick fury at Derek's reply but just as quickly a vile smile spread across her face as she cradled her growing belly. The act made Derek sick.

"No," she purred, "Let's play twenty questions... you get to go first."

Derek stood staring at Daria in confusion.

"Ask me a question!" she stomped her feet in a small fit of rage.

Derek blinked for a moment before asking, "Okay. Why? Why are you doing this to me?"

Daria smiled widely with approval, "Yes! Good... good question. Well, I think my answer should be very clear. I mean..." she looked down, continuing to cradle her womb.

"No," Derek shook his head. "You could've done *that* with any human... And, as disgusting as it sounds, there are some men, apparently, that would volunteer. Why me?"

"That's question two," Daria started to pace a small path between Derek and Alexis. She placed her hand thoughtfully on her chin, "Why you? Because you're special."

"Special? How?" he continued.

"Hmmm...is that two more questions? Are we up to four now?" Daria winked at Alexis who smiled broadly, "I think we are."

"Daria," Derek demanded with impatience, his gun still pointed at her head. She was really starting to get on his nerves.

"Oh, lover," she cooed, "You will allow me a little latitude. Or I'll make sure your precious little Siobhan starts living another nightmare."

She gave a glaring look over at Alexis who yanked hard on Siobhan's auburn waves, moving his hand a little closer to her face.

"Don't do it," Derek warned Alexis.

Daria howled with laughter, "Oh! This is fun! Will Derek shoot me or Alexis? Will he save himself or his little friend? Now that's a game!"

"Daria. How am I special?" Much like how adults ignore unpleasant behaviors in children, Derek did his best to ignore Daria's. He wanted to keep her on task and get the answers he wanted.

"Oh, boo... Back to that? Well, okay...but let's hurry this along. I have preparations to complete, and I need you dead."

She smiled sweetly at Derek, continuing, "You're special because of your bloodline."

"My bloodline? Look lady, I'm an orphan. You've clearly got your wires crossed," he laughed derisively.

Daria's amusement was palpable, "I am in awe as to how stupid you are, human. It's been in front of you this whole time and you still refuse to see it."

She looked wide-eyed at Alexis and asked, "Can I now love?"

Alexis grinned from ear to ear and nodded slowly.

Daria could hardly contain her excitement, "Oh, Derek... You carry royal blood."

"Oh lady, you really are crazy... *You* think I'm royalty? Sure. Okay. So, what? Queen Elizabeth is my grandmother?" Derek laughed wildly.

"Oh my God. Really stupid," Daria rolled her eyes. "I'm talking about actual royalty. Not what your Known thinks are royalty. Royalty with *real* power...and..." Daria's voice lifted in a teasing tone, "...You've even met your mother. Been spending a lot of time with her, I hear."

Derek was frozen in place. His *mother*. The only memories of a mother figure were from the few foster homes he remembered as a very young child, before his placement in the orphanage. He'd given up on a family years before. He couldn't even imagine it. Was Daria, right? Did he really have a mother and even a father out in the world somewhere?

In a flash, he thought about everyone he had ever met...could one of those women be his mother? What about recently? Who had he met that would be the right age and fit as his mother? Realization washed over him like a waterfall, and it didn't go unnoticed by anyone in the room.

"Ahhh... There it is," Daria shrieked with glee. "Yes, the one and only son of Julia Silverlight."

Derek shook his head in disagreement, "No... That can't be true."

"It is. And you know it," Daria roared angrily. "You remember I've seen inside your mind. You know there are secrets that are being kept from you. Well... there it is... you have your answer."

"Okay, if it is true, why keep it from me? Why abandon me to this world? Wouldn't my father have some say? And..." the questions rolled from Derek's tongue with quick ease, "...How do you know any of this?"

"Five, six, seven, eight," she counted out loud as she paced the floor again. "Now, I can't tell you about the motivations behind your mother's decision. I mean, I would never leave my child behind," she resumed rubbing her stomach. "But, contrary to popular belief, I'm not a selfish bitch."

Siobhan chuckled as Alexis wove his fingers tighter in her hair. Daria's head snapped in her direction, but she quickly returned her attention to Derek.

"As for your father..." Daria's oily smile returned, sliding slowly across her pale face, "Well, let's just say your mother's consort was a weak man. I know this because I'm the one that tortured him until he gave me what I wanted."

Once again, her raucous laughter filled the space.

Fury began building inside Derek again. He was so angry at Daria for doing this to him, but he was even angrier at Julia for hiding this secret the entire time. He glanced over at Siobhan who was still sitting uncomfortably on her knees, her head tilted slightly back at Alexis' feet. He had to think of her right now and remain calm. Otherwise, neither one of them would make it out of this warehouse alive.

He took a deep breath and continued, "I get it now... You think having a child of royal blood will put you on the throne in the Hidden... that's actually a little pathetic."

Daria's eyes flashed icy blue, glaring at Derek, "Pathetic? I will put the Succubae in their rightful place."

"Rightful place? Aren't you all just bastard children? I'm pretty sure royalty is mostly purebred," Derek stated as a matter of fact.

"We are not bastards!" she screamed ferociously.

Derek noticed the warehouse had gotten brighter in the last ten minutes and he decided that it was time to execute his and Siobhan's plan. Surely the Forhelien had discovered he was gone by now. And he knew it wouldn't take much more to get Daria over the edge; he just had to keep pushing.

"So, what is your plan? Kill me and use my life force to have *that*?" he pointed to her belly. "But, beyond that, what? Julia will never recognize an illegitimate child from a race that is too full of themselves to live under a treaty."

"She will have no choice," Daria growled, her perfect stony teeth barred.

Derek knew he had her. She was the one on the defensive now and he knew he only had to push a few more buttons. Without looking away from Daria, he nodded his head slightly to signal to Siobhan they were almost ready.

"Well, you're wrong. Look at it, Daria. The ones that have signed the treaty are all pureblood, right? They don't really want you or your kind around, let alone in power. I mean, can you blame them? A bloodthirsty, psychopathic, half-breed?" he challenged.

Daria's roaring scream was only silenced by the gunfire heard outside of the large entrance doors. The next few actions only took seconds to complete.

Siobhan pulled her head down abruptly to knock Alexis off his center of gravity while simultaneously reaching behind her back to pull out the tiny handgun Derek had given her. She raised it over her head and placed the muzzle directly under his chin, pulling the trigger. There was no blood from her angle, but steam began to waft out of the entrance wound, a side effect of the sanctified bullet.

Daria wailed and spat with crazed fury and started across the room at Siobhan, but Derek's bullet was faster. Her head loped forward then back again mere milliseconds after Siobhan's gun went off. Daria fell silent dropping to the hard concrete, blood, and steam seeping from her brain.

Derek and Siobhan remained still for several moments staring at what had transpired. Random gunfire and yelling were heard clearly right outside the warehouse door. Derek made his way over to Siobhan, leaned over, and helped her to her feet. The tussle with Alexis had twisted her leg and she was having some difficulty standing. Derek holstered his gun behind his back, wrapping his arm around her waist, helping to steady her.

26

Both groups of Forhelien fought their way to either end of the warehouse to gain access. Time seemed at a standstill. Casius and his group finally eliminated the succubae holding the hallway and once they were dead, the demons immediately disappeared into thin air.

"Cowards!" Abhainn laughed loudly as the last demon bared its teeth, shimmering into nothing.

Casius was already working on access through the large double doors. Making a fist with his extremely large hand, he squared his shoulder where the doors met, drew back, and hit hard. The lock made an audible *pop* as both doors flew open.

He motioned for Zhaar to go in first and the lanky Fae swiftly moved past him stopping short. Abhainn and Casius followed close behind and nearly ran into the white-haired fae.

"We're too late," Zhaar's large eyes widened.

The trio of soldiers stared at the scene in front of them. Derek was assisting Siobhan off the concrete floor with Daria and Alexis lying dead at their feet. Just then, one of the bay doors rose to the ceiling. Casius and Abhainn aimed their weapons, but quickly lowered them again as Julia, Captain Vena, and Alder stood on the threshold.

Siobhan limped lightly as she and Derek moved toward the risen bay door. On the other side stood more Forhelien and a dozen Brethren; all with guns and arrows drawn in defensive positions. Vena looked from Derek to Siobhan and then to the bodies of the dead succubae on the ground. She smiled proudly at Derek, nodding once sharply in approval.

Derek and Siobhan turned, making their way down the dock ramp to the outside, and stood in front of the group. He stared hard at Julia but said nothing. He didn't know exactly what to say and whatever it was would've been in anger. His *mother*. He really didn't care if he ever saw her again. *She* made the decision to leave *him*; why would he ever forgive that? Could he forgive that? He stared for another moment then turned his head and unlocked their gaze. He helped Siobhan into a nearby van and told the Brethren' driver to get out.

Pulling out of the building's parking lot, they noticed that it was crawling with Forhelien and Brethren soldiers. It was finally over. Derek turned away from the scene and never checked the rearview mirror.

27

Derek sat for the first time in over two weeks alone in his own apartment. He felt like a stranger to it. It was almost midnight and he had just stepped out of what he thought was the best shower he had ever taken. After he and Siobhan left the warehouse, they made their way back to the Forhelien safe house, gathered their belongings, and called for a cab.

They made it back to Siobhan's apartment before the first of the Brethren began to arrive back from the siege. He helped Siobhan into her living room and get settled. He told her he really thought he needed to be alone and wanted to see what his place looked like since it had been a while. She agreed that they both could use hot showers and the comfort of their own beds. He promised he would call her and left.

Now he sat on the edge of his bed, naked, save for the towel that circled his waist, wondering what to do from here. He wanted to call Siobhan and talk to her. She wanted to talk earlier today, but he shut her out. Now, he was desperate to hear her voice. She always could talk him through the ideas that ran in his head, but the thoughts now were so large, so overwhelming. He had a family, at least a mother, and from the sound of it, his father was dead at the hands of Daria.

Daria called him the only son. Was he an only child, or did he have siblings? What did it mean to be a son of a witch queen? He chuckled to himself because it sounded like an insult. It also felt unreal and ridiculous. He ran his hands through his wet dark hair and sighed. He lay back on the bed and continued his inner familial monologue. What did this all mean? He lay there only for a few minutes when a soft knock rapped on his front door.

Siobhan.

He threw on a shirt and basketball shorts as he made his way through the apartment. The gun he had *borrowed* from the armory was on his bookshelf and he picked it up as he walked by. If it wasn't her, he would be ready. He held it with the safety off in his right hand, looking through the peephole. He sighed, unlocked the deadbolt and chain, and opened the door to Julia standing in the hallway.

"I really don't have anything to say to you... I thought I made that clear this morning," he said as he left the door open and walked over to his sofa, sitting, gun still in hand.

"May I come in, my child?" Julia asked softly.

Derek laughed wryly, "Ha. *My child*... I guess you're going to say that you didn't lie to me or conceal the truth... *My child*."

The words were bitter tasting as they dropped off his tongue.

Julia, who was dressed in a more casual style of long gray slacks, a white blouse, and an expensive-looking black leather jacket, carried something small in her arms. She stepped over the threshold, closing the door behind her. She walked over to the edge of the sofa and sat softly on the arm, careful not to get too close to Derek out of respect.

She folded her hands in her lap over the item she was carrying and took a deep breath, "I know that I will never be able to apologize enough for not being straightforward with you. It's completely unacceptable, but I *am* very sorry for the pain I've caused."

"Pain? There's no pain... Frustration? Yes. Anger? Hell yes. But pain?" Derek's voice was angry but steady.

"Derek…" Julia hung her head in contemplation of what she would say next.

"You know what, *Mom*? Save it. I really don't want to hear anything you have to say," he interrupted her.

For the first time since their first meeting, Julia raised her voice at him, "I know what I've done is wrong. I know that I lied to you. But you will allow me to say my peace and offer some semblance of understanding. What you choose to do with it is on you. I don't expect you to forgive me, but I do expect you to be fair to me!"

Derek glowered at her but said nothing.

"I did hide you away… I wanted you to live a normal life in the Known and not a life of servitude to the Hidden as the next in line to the throne. I remember being that child…I remember how I felt to always have the burden of service hung on me. I didn't want that for you. It was my choice, one that others in my family have made. Your father…well…" she choked on the words that stuck in her throat.

"Your father was the love of my life. He promised to make sure you had a wonderful life here but, then Daria took *him* away. I honestly thought I had lost you forever. It took me years to find you, but by the time I did…well, look at you! You're a grown man… you've done so much with your life, and I didn't think I could inject myself like that. I wanted you to have peace."

"I take responsibility for what has happened," she continued. "Daria and I have been at odds since I was a young novice. But Derek…you did something I couldn't… you defeated her. You have so much power within you…and your aura pulses with it. I believe it's what helped you survive against her."

A long pause fell between the pair.

"Just so you know, my life hasn't always been so *peaceful*," Derek interjected quietly. "I moved from foster home to foster home.… No one wanted me. Do you know what that does to a little kid? Finally, I went to the orphanage, which wasn't all fun and games either... I got knocked around pretty good by the older kids... until I could fight back. Then at eighteen, you know what happens? I was kicked out... You're an adult suddenly and are expected to immediately act like one. I've worked my ass off for everything I have...no thanks to you."

"I am so sorry... I wish you had never experienced those things," Julia whispered. There was another long pause between mother and son.

"What was his name?" Derek asked softly.

"What?" Julia replied with slight confusion.

"My father. What was his name?" he asked again, harder.

"Richard... His name was Richard," Julia hung her head as a single tear fell off her chin.

"So, what now? Where does this leave me?" Derek asked with a voice that could cut stone even though his heart began to soften at the sight of her pain.

"How do you mean?"

"I mean, what do I do now? Do I come with you? Does my life change? Apparently, I'm now... what? A prince of some sort?" He asked.

Julia took a deep breath and smiled at her son, "What you do with this is up to you. No one will force you to change any part of your life... I *would* like to be a part of it, of course...if, someday you can allow that. Please know that the Order is appreciative of what you've done. You will always have a home in the Hidden if you choose."

As if looking at her for the first time, Derek noticed how similar he and Julia were and he wondered why he hadn't seen it until now. They had the same hairline, and her eyes were the same tone of amber as his. Their body shape was also very similar as they were both very tall for their respective genders and carried lean muscle. The realization made Derek feel more conflicting emotions that he was still unable to process. He decided to put those aside and just focus on being angry with her.

"It doesn't matter. Right now, we're still strangers and I'm not sure what any of this will mean down the road." Rising from his seat, he walked to the door, "Look, I think I've got to get out of here for a while and need some sleep before I leave."

Julia gazed at him but didn't move from her perch, "Of course. I'm sure you have a lot to think about. Just one more question…"

"Shoot."

"What about Siobhan?" she asked pointedly.

The mere mention of Siobhan's name sent butterflies through him. But it also angered him more to hear Julia talk about her as her secrets could've gotten Siobhan killed.

"What about her?" he responded harshly.

"Have you discussed your feelings with her?"

"You haven't come up… she understands that I need some time," he shrugged.

Julia sighed, shaking her head, "No… your feelings for *her*."

Derek could feel his cheeks flush. He was trying to avoid thinking about that also. Deep down, he knew he loved her, and he knew the exact moment he fell in love with her. If he were being honest with himself, he couldn't get her off his mind, which was another tiny reason he needed to get away for a few days. He needed to sort out his feeling about the situation with Julia and figure out a way of telling Siobhan exactly how he felt about her and their relationship. All without scaring her or pissing her off.

His physical response was noticed by Julia and a soft smile moved across her face, "Son…"

"No! You don't get to call me that," he snapped, throwing himself out of his seat.

She held her hands up in surrender, "You're right. I was out of line... I apologize."

Derek stared hard at her.

"But about Siobhan," she continued, "I think if you reflect on it, you'll find your feelings for her are pure. You shouldn't be afraid of them... I feel you've had them for a long time and longer than you realize. I think you'll find that the stress of this past week only worked to solidify what was already forged. You both are two sides of the same coin...you can't have one without the other."

Standing to leave, she handed Derek the item she carried with her. Siobhan's maroon hoodie was folded neatly into a small rectangle, "I think this was left behind."

Derek took the sweater, "Thanks."

Julia nodded and walked out of the apartment. Derek returned to the sofa and slumped down in its deep cushions. He put the shirt to his nose and took a deep breath.

28

— • —

The next morning, the cloudy Portland skies found Siobhan pacing around her living room with earbuds dangled from her head.

"C'mon Theo, pick up," she said to the ringing phone.

She disconnected the call before it went to voicemail, deciding she would just go to the studio instead and see if she could find Derek there. She tried all morning to get a hold of him, but he didn't answer his phone or return a text message. She thought a quick call to Theo might help, but it was clear that neither of them could be reached.

She wasn't particularly worried about Derek as he made it very clear with the events of the day prior that he could take care of himself. But she also knew that he must be reeling from the shock of learning that he had a *mother*. And not just a mother, but a mother that was the head of the supernatural otherworld. She couldn't imagine where his head was at right now, but her mind wasn't exactly straight either. The past week had been an enormous emotional drain on her, and she hadn't rested the night before. She ran every detail over in her mind all night. At about three a.m. she started to piece together and recognize things that she had overlooked before.

The nightmare she had during her capture by Daria and Alexis was at the forefront of her thoughts. The picture of Derek lying bloody and dying was one she would never forget. She could still feel the stickiness and the warmth of his blood as it dripped through her fingers. As the memories of that horrific dream played in her head, her heart began to race again. Her worst fear played out in front of her, and she couldn't stop it. Derek had killed himself. The one person she respected and cared for the most in the whole world was gone. She had a difficult time shaking the dream off.

There were so many things she wanted to tell him, things that she'd been carrying around for more than a year and never had the guts to say out loud. But that dream was a farce and a bastardization of an actual event that occurred a long time before she even knew Derek. The question that lingered in her mind was: what exactly was reality now?

She knew that Derek must have also had some pretty intense night terrors while Asha poisoned him at the safe house. The very first night he looked like he had been crying and practically smothered her in a bear hug. Siobhan had to wonder if that dream was about her. Were the feelings she was having for him just a manifestation of her protectiveness of him? She vetoed that thought almost immediately.

She had always been protective of their friendship, but over the past year, she had been pushing her attraction to him deeper inside. She remembered the nervous excitement she felt every time he was near her in recent days. Was all this just Daria's torture? Was this just another implanted false memory? She thought back to their last conversation at that ornate table; her heart raced as she thought again about his fingertips on her cheek. She remembered the disappointment she felt when Casius walked in, and Derek backed away. She thought he may have kissed her then.

Now, in the light of day, she felt stupid and ridiculous. Derek was safe and alive, and Daria was dead. She would no longer be a threat to any of them. Maybe now she could finally tell Derek how she felt about him; how she *really* felt. But something different and darker was still eating its way through Siobhan's thoughts, and it had nothing to do with Derek, not really. It was an emotion that she was all too familiar with these past few days and that feeling was fury.

Siobhan and Julia had been friends for several years and a feeling of betrayal was beginning to build inside of her. How could Julia do this to her? How could she do this to Derek? Was their friendship also a lie? One that would get Julia closer to Derek? Siobhan didn't like lies as a general rule, but the basket of deceit that Julia had woven was astronomical. There were so many things she wanted to ask and so many things she wanted to say to Julia, but it was all too much right now. She couldn't dwell on those emotions at the present moment. Right now, what she needed was to make sure Derek was in a good headspace and for all of them to get back to normal. There were bigger tasks to take deal with and life to get back to. She decided to pack those thoughts away, for now, get dressed, and make her way to work.

She arrived an hour later to find the lights off and the doors locked tight. It was still over an hour before they should have opened so that was not even unusual. She did find it a little weird that the *Closed for Vacation* note was still attached to the front window. She quietly unlocked the door but once inside she could smell freshly brewed coffee wafting from the small beverage station behind the front desk.

"Derek?" she called out. She heard a chair slide and footsteps fall, but to her disappointment, Theo walked out of one of the session rooms. Siobhan's heart sank.

"Hey! How are you?" Theo smiled with his signature good attitude and made to give her a hug.

"Oh, hey Theo. Sorry, I thought maybe Derek was here," Siobhan found it hard to hide her discouragement.

Theo frowned, "Nah, just me. He stopped by earlier...said he would be away for a few more days."

"Away? Away where?" she pressed.

"No idea, he didn't say... but he left you a note," Theo shrugged, pointing to her desk.

"Oh...okay," Siobhan began to feel a little hurt that he hadn't confided in her about his plans. "I guess I'll get some work done then."

At the moment she sat, Siobhan's phone rang, and Derek's picture popped up on the screen. She smiled to herself, and her heart leaped a little.

"Hello?" she answered quickly.

"Hey...it's me. Did you get my note?" Derek's voice was soft as he spoke.

"I actually just got here.... What's going on?" Siobhan asked, concerned.

"Everything's okay, I promise. I really..." his voice stumbled, "Julia came to see me last night. Von, I need to clear my head... I'm not good to anyone right now...especially you. I just need a couple of days to wrap my head around some stuff."

Siobhan knew he was right, and her heart broke for him. She wished that she could set everything right for him. But just like he knew months ago that Siobhan would need to heal herself, she knew now that Derek would have to do the same.

"Okay," she replied, "But if you need anything, you'll call?"

"I'll only be gone a couple of days... I promise, I'll call... see you soon," Derek said as he hung up.

Siobhan sat her phone down still disheartened but finally gave in to starting her day.

***

The next few days rolled by slowly for Siobhan as the monotony of life drug on without event and her anxiety quietly grew. Wake, work, home, then little sleep. There was a missing piece from her existence, and it was clear what that was. After three days, and still no word from Derek, Siobhan was more tense than she had been in months. He told her he would be gone *a couple of days* and that he would call. Three passed, and still no word from him. So many thoughts ran through her head but none of them kept her from missing him and she desperately wanted to make sure he was alright. At one point, she even considered calling Julia to find out if she had heard from him. Maybe he was trying to work things out in the Hidden with his new family. The thought was quickly lost when she realized she couldn't bear to speak to Julia yet because she was still fiercely angry with her.

When Saturday finally arrived, she and Theo decided to close the shop early that night because business was slow most of the day. In their brief absence, Theo started dating a new woman and had an extreme *"need"* to spend time with his new girl. Siobhan knew that was Theo-speak for wanting to get laid and she laughed at him relentlessly about his long line of euphemisms for sex. But she agreed that it was a waste of money to keep the doors open and felt she deserved a night of relaxation that hopefully led to a good night's sleep.

It was somewhere around nine o'clock when she found herself lying on the overstuffed sofa in her apartment. Her small Chinese takeout box was open but empty on the table in front of her, chopsticks tossed inside. Light flickered softly and long shadows were cast by the candles she lit throughout the space and soft Neo-soul music hung in the air. She put her book down, leaned her head back, closing her eyes. She couldn't remember the last time she was able to just *be* in her own space. She hoped that Derek was also feeling some peace, wherever he was. God knows they both needed and deserved it.

Siobhan walked to the kitchen to pour herself a glass of water. She opened the freezer, reaching in for a few cubes of ice when she saw it; the paper bag was still folded over and crimped at the top of the small package. She smiled to herself as she remembered the mint chip ice cream Derek brought her as an apology days earlier. It was her favorite of any other flavor, and the image of his sweet gesture brought a now familiar pang to her heart. Where could he be? She missed him so much. The thought of another day without him seemed to make her more miserable. She pulled the pint out of the freezer and found a spoon.

She only took a couple of bites when the alarm on her intercom buzzed. She walked to the black box beside the door and pushed the button to talk.

"Who is it?" she asked.

"Von, it's me," Derek's voice rang clear over the speaker.

A large lump immediately formed in her throat and her heart started beating wildly. Her stomach rolled as she tried to catch her breath and she found, to her surprise, that she was also now concurrently furious with him. Where the hell had he been? What was he doing here?

"Yeah?" was the only word she managed to choke out.

"Can I come up?" he asked.

Siobhan considered herself for a moment, she wasn't exactly dressed to take visitors. So many thoughts ran in her mind. How could she feel both excited and mad at the same time?

"Von?" he asked, wondering if she was still there.

"Where have you been?" she croaked out, still fighting to keep the tears from falling.

Derek recognized her tone of voice and hung his head in shame. He had hurt her again and knew it immediately.

"I had to clear my head. I went up to Oxbow to spend a few days alone. Look, I know you're upset, and you have every right to be... I promise I'll explain everything, just please let me in." He paused looking down at his hands then added, "I have something for you..."

Siobhan looked down at the ice cream but remained silent.

"Von, please," he pleaded. "I know I should've called. You know how service can be there...but it was still a dick move. I just needed to sort things out in my head. Look, I think we have to talk...we have so much to talk about."

If she demanded him to crawl on his knees begging for forgiveness, he would. But after several silent moments of dead air, he heard the lock release.

Derek again took the stairs two at a time as he set out in an almost dead run up the risers. As he reached the third-floor landing, he noticed Siobhan had cracked the door open for him already. He pushed it wide and saw her standing with her back to him. She was dressed in black Capri workout pants and a gray hoodie. Her long auburn hair fell to the middle of her back, and she was barefoot. From where he stood, he saw the strongest and most beautiful woman in the world.

Siobhan turned to face him, the tears running like a stream down her pale face. She wanted to be as angry with him right now as she had been in the last few minutes, but when she saw him, her heart melted and all of it went away. Her attraction to him was like an explosion of worlds, and her knees buckled when she looked at him.

He wore dark jeans and a stylish gray button-down shirt that he left stylishly untucked. He was clean-shaven except for his goatee and mustache, and he finally got a haircut. She could smell the clean scent of his cologne from where she stood, and it was intoxicating. In his hand, he carried a small bouquet of wildflowers with a single pink rose at its center. Siobhan's heart pounded like a drum, and she thought for a moment it would jump out of her chest. He was certainly dressed to kill.

The two stared at each other for several moments. Derek's head shook at her as he closed the space between them in three large paces. He dropped the flowers, wrapped her up in his arms, and pulled her in, kissing her slowly and deliberately. Siobhan's body fell into him and surrendered. Heat rose inside them both as they embraced each other tightly; neither was willing to give the other up.

Their kiss finally came to a natural stopping point and Derek looked down into Siobhan's glistening emerald eyes.

"I am so sorry," he apologized quietly. "I had so many things to work out and thought that I was better doing that on my own.... I realized yesterday that I was so wrong. I understand that a lot of the darkness I've been feeling was because I had been ignoring what was in front of me.... Von, I can't live without you... I think I've known that for a very long time. Ignoring what I felt for you pushed me into that meeting with Daria.... I'm so sorry I've been such a shit and didn't...."

He shook his head looking for the right words, "By the time I was ready...We were too deep in what was going on and there had already been too many lies...too much confusion...too much manipulation."

He brushed a lone tear from her cheek, "I was never confused... Never. I just didn't think you felt the same way...but I can't live that lie anymore... I only want you in my life."

Siobhan took a small, shaky breath, "Derek... I'm not sure what to say."

"It's okay... Please say anything Von... Please say you felt this too...I can't be this far off base...I'm not, am I?" Derek's words were replaced by another kiss from her. She wrapped her arms around his neck, running her hands through his dark, freshly styled hair.

She pulled away slowly, brushing his pillowed lips with hers. "I was afraid that...*I* was the only one that felt it," her voice trembled as another tear ran down her cheek.

"That night that Daria took me from the safe house...the only thing I dreamt of was you," she began but held back the actuality of the nightmare that the succubus created.

"I woke up and thought I had missed my chance with you," she paused a moment. "Do you remember that night I stayed at your apartment, the night that Paul and I split?"

"I do," Derek replied, stroking her hair.

"That moment... You did everything you could think of to make everything right...but it was when you just let me fall apart and just held me and listened...I knew...how... I really felt," Siobhan's voice shook nervously and she blushed.

Derek pulled her tighter against him, "That was months ago," he whispered.

The gravity of her words was still sinking in as he continued, "She picked memories that meant something to both of us and tried to use them against us... Von, don't allow her to exist there anymore... remember, she's gone and never coming back. She wanted to fuck with our heads."

He paused, "That night was special to me too."

Their faces were only millimeters apart.

"What do you mean?" Siobhan asked quietly. She could feel his warm breath on her cheek.

"Because every time I think about it..." He hung his head, pausing again, "It's the first night I can remember feeling..."

"We were something else...more than friends," Siobhan finished for him.

Derek nodded, "Yeah."

"I didn't want to leave your side...I felt safe and like it was normal. The way it was supposed to be," waves of relief cascaded over her, and the tears streaked faster down her now rosy cheeks, "I thought it was just me."

Derek sighed, shaking his head, "Oh my God, Von... no...not just you...if we could go back...I'd never let you leave."

He fell into her eyes again and kissed her soft lips.

"I...I hate it when you cry," his dark eyes moved gently over hers.

Siobhan gave him a small laugh, hanging her head, "I know."

He hooked his finger under her chin and lifted her face toward him. He studied it, running his hand softly over her cheek again.

"I don't know what happens now or where this thing with Julia and the Hidden is going.... all things we'll deal with...*together.* The only thing I want to do right now," he studied her eyes a little more and said softly, "I love you."

Derek's lips met hers once again.

ABOUT THE AUTHOR

January Kelly is a longtime writer and holds a BS in Sociology with an interest in Religious Studies. She is an avid reader of fantasy and science fiction and a lover of all genres of music. January is based in the wilds of the Missouri Midwest where she loves to embroider bad words on bookmarks, have cocktails and queso with her friends, and go on long walks with her husband, Jarritt.

www.januarykelly.com
Follow on Facebook:
https://www.facebook.com/profile.php?id=100067850730415
Instagram:
https://www.instagram.com/januarykelly.author/?next=%2F

Paranormal Romantic Suspense

The Hidden Series:

The Night They Knew- a short story from The Hidden

Hidden Intent

Smoke and Shadow

Relative Deceit—coming soon!

Standalone:

The Last Lament of the Late Shawn Reilly

Contemporary Fiction

All These Days

www.ingramcontent.com/pod-product-compliance
Lightning Source LLC
Chambersburg PA
CBHW020114310726
48970CB00002B/626